To William

Wishing you a Merry Christmas

From Mr & Mrs Bodman.

ENID BLYTON'S
FIRESIDE TALES

Enid Blyton's
FIRESIDE
TALES

COLLINS
LONDON AND GLASGOW

This Impression 1968

PRINTED AND MADE IN GREAT BRITAIN BY
WM. COLLINS SONS AND CO. LTD.
LONDON AND GLASGOW

CONTENTS

The Little Candy House

ONCE upon a time there were two little girls, one called Rosalind and one called Rosemary. They lived in a cottage with their father and mother, and helped their mother in her work.

Rosemary was sweet and merry, but Rosalind was sulky and bad-tempered. She teased her sister, and often made her unhappy. Rosemary was never unkind, but sometimes her merry face grew sad when Rosalind pulled her hair and pinched her. She often did her sister's work for her, but Rosalind never thanked her or did her a good deed in return.

One day it was baking day and the girls' mother told them to bake bread, cakes and tarts.

"I have to go out to-day," she said, "and I want you two girls to finish the baking for me. You must each do half, and when I come home, it must all be finished."

She put on her hat and coat and went out. Rosalind at once made a horrid face at Rosemary.

"*You* can do all the work!" she said. "I'm going to read my book."

"No, Rosalind, you really must help me," said Rosemary. "I shall never get it all done by myself. There is such a lot to do."

But Rosalind sat down in a corner and wouldn't lift a finger. Rosemary sighed and set to work. She was a good little baker. Rosalind was a bad cook— she let the cakes burn and the tarts grow as black as cinders. As for her bread, it was horrid.

Rosemary worked hard all the day. The baking was only done once a fortnight, so there was a lot to do. She made two big fruit tarts, twenty little jam tarts, an apple pudding, four cakes and thirty little buns, as well as baking many loaves of bread. Rosalind wouldn't even help to wash up the dirty dishes.

Rosemary felt cross. She so often did Rosalind's work, and she was getting tired of it.

"Rosalind," she said, as she put away the last dish, "you are very selfish. This is the last time I shall do your work for you. When our mother comes home I shall tell her that you sat in a corner and read all day and that I have done everything. It is not fair for you to take half the praise when you have done nothing at all."

Then Rosalind flew into a temper. She rushed at Rosemary, pulled her hair, pinched her arm, and kicked her on the ankle. Then she took the apple pudding and flung it on the floor so that it smashed into pulp.

"*I* shall tell our mother that *you* spoilt the pudding!" said Rosalind, angrily. "So there! If you are going to tell tales, I shall too!"

Rosemary was so upset when she saw her lovely pudding on the floor that she burst into tears and ran straight out of the house. She went to the woods and followed a path there, winding in and out of the trees till she came to a little dell she knew. Then she sat down and wept bitterly. It was too bad of Rosalind to be so horrid.

Soon she got up and began to walk through the wood once more.

She thought she was taking the homeward path, but because of her tears, she took the wrong one, and soon she was lost.

She stood beneath an oak tree, wondering which way to go. She was very hungry, for she had eaten nothing since she had begun her work that morning. She wandered on, looking for some sign of a woodman's cottage, so that she might ask her way.

Suddenly she came to a little clearing, and in the middle of it stood the queerest cottage she had ever seen. Its walls were made of currant cake, trimmed with little jam tarts, its windows were outlined in bars of chocolate, the chimneys were of gingerbread, the doorsteps were of toffee and the door was studded with chocolate buns.

"Well!" said Rosemary, in surprise. "What a

funny house! It's made of cakes, tarts, chocolate and candy! I wonder who lives there."

She went up to the door and knocked. No one came to open it and Rosemary knocked again. Still no one came, and when the little girl tried the handle she found that the door was fast shut.

She was disappointed, and tears came into her eyes again. She had so hoped to find someone there who could tell her the way home. She sat down on the doorstep and waited. Soon the smell of the cottage tickled her nose—it was a lovely smell of newly made cake, chocolate and candy.

"Surely it wouldn't matter if I ate just a little bit of the house," thought Rosemary. "I *am* so hungry. There's this little jam tart here—it looks so nice."

She broke off a small jam tart and ate it hungrily. Then she took a little cake and broke off a bit of chocolate too, to eat with it. How good it all was!

But suddenly she jumped up, startled. An angry voice came from the cottage and frightened Rosemary.

"Who is eating my candy house? How dare you, how dare you!"

"Please, I'm very sorry," said Rosemary. "I was very hungry. I did knock twice but nobody came."

"Well, how was I to know you weren't a robber!" said the scolding voice, and the door flew open. In the entrance stood a witch-woman, very bent and old, with a tall pointed hat. She shook her fist at Rosemary and grabbed her by the arm.

"You come indoors with me, and I'll see what punishment you shall have for picking at my house like that!" said the old dame. "Dear, dear, to think it was only last week I baked all those things and made myself a nice little candy house, and now here comes a nasty little girl who thinks it is only made for eating."

"Do forgive me," begged Rosemary. "Won't you let me make you a few jam tarts and cakes, and then you can trim up your house again? I can bake quite well, really I can."

"No girls bake properly nowadays," grumbled the old woman. "Sit down child. Why, you're shivering! Come to the fire and I will make you a pot of tea. I can see you will try to make up for pulling my house to pieces."

Soon Rosemary was sitting by the fire and drinking hot tea. She was not so frightened of the old dame now, but she really was very sorry that she had upset her so much.

"It is getting dark now, and I shall never find my way home to-night," said Rosemary. "If you would be kind enough to let me stay with you for the night, old dame, I will be up early to-morrow and do any baking you want done."

"Very well," said the witch-woman. "I will see how you can cook. But woe betide you if you do badly!"

She made up a bed for Rosemary by the fire, and very soon there was nothing to be heard in the little candy house but the fall of the wood in the fire. The old dame had gone to her bed in the room off the kitchen, and Rosemary, tired out, was fast asleep.

Early next morning, before the old woman was awake, Rosemary slipped from her bed. She made it neatly and folded up the rug. Then she dressed herself and went to the cupboard to see what the old woman had there. There was flour, sugar, butter and milk, and everything else that Rosemary needed for baking. She made up the fire and peeped inside the oven. Now she would begin her work!

It was very early. The old woman still slept in the little bedroom. Rosemary worked hard. She made some beautiful jam tarts, and some dear little chocolate buns with coconut on the top. Then she thought that perhaps the old witch would like an apple pudding for her breakfast and she made one of her very best.

She peeped into the little bedroom. The dame was just stirring. Rosemary slipped back into the kitchen and made a pot of tea. She put it on a tray and crept into the bedroom.

"Are you awake, dame?" she asked. "Here is some tea for you."

"Well, well!" said the witch, sitting up in surprise. "What a nice kind girl!"

"I've done all the baking," said Rosemary. "And I made an apple pudding for you, dame. Would you like some for your breakfast? It's just ready."

"I could just fancy a taste of apple pudding," said the old woman. "But there's few that can make it to my liking, maiden. Bring it in."

When the witch saw the fine apple pudding she was delighted. She ate some and said it was just as good as hers. She and Rosemary finished it together, and soon they were very good friends.

"Now let me see what work you have done this morning," said the old dame, and she trotted out to the kitchen. Wasn't she pleased when she saw all Rosemary's lovely tarts and cakes!

"Why, you're as good a cook as I am myself!" she cried. "A maid like you would make a good little wife. You should wed a prince, for you're worth your weight in gold!"

Rosemary cleaned the little cottage well, and then she asked the old witch if she might go.

"Yes," said the old woman, "though I'm sorry to part with you, my dear, you're such a merry, hard-working little maid. Wait! Before you go, you shall have a present."

She went to a drawer and took out a little box. In it were some brooches. Some were of gold, and looked rich. Others were ordinary, set in the shape of birds.

"Choose which you would like," said the old woman.

Rosemary did not like to take a gold one, for she was only a peasant maid. Besides, she could not choose the best there, that would be greedy. So she took a little brown brooch in the form of a tiny bird.

"Thank you very much," she said, and she pinned it to her dress.

"It is a cold day and you have no cloak," said the witch. "You shall have one of mine. See, which will you have?"

She took the girl to where six cloaks hung in a row. They were all turned inside out so that only their linings showed. There were two lined with gold, one with silver, and one with silk. The others were lined with cloth and one was rather torn.

"I'll have this one," said Rosemary, taking the torn one. "I cannot take your good ones, dame —you are too kind to me."

"Come and see me again one day," said the old woman, and kissed Rosemary lovingly. Then she told her the way to go home. The little girl ran off happily, the warm cloak round her shoulders—but when she came into the sunshine, she stopped in astonishment! The cloak might have a torn cloth lining—but the outer side was of shimmering gold! Diamonds shone here and there and rows of pearls trimmed the neck.

"Well!" cried Rosemary in wonder. "I chose the oldest—and it is the best of the lot! Whatever will my mother say?"

Soon she was home—but her mother greeted her with scolding words and frowns.

"You naughty girl, where have you been all this time? How dare you leave your sister to do all that baking and how wicked of you to throw the pudding on the floor!"

"Mother, Mother, I didn't!" cried Rosemary. "*I* did all the baking! And it was Rosalind who spoilt the pudding!"

But her mother did not believe her. Rosemary ran away and sat down sadly by the well. Why, her mother had been so angry she had not even noticed her lovely cloak!

As the girl looked at it, her spirits rose and she felt happy again. Suddenly she felt as if she must sing, and she opened her mouth—and lo and behold, she carolled as sweetly as a nightingale! The brown bird on the little brooch she had chosen was a magic nightingale, and whoever wore the brooch had the gift of song.

So sweet was Rosemary's voice that everyone gathered round to listen. Suddenly there came the sound of a horse, and who should ride up but the prince of that land, very straight and handsome.

When he saw the pretty maiden sitting there in her glittering cloak, singing sweetly as a nightingale, he straightway fell in love with her.

"You shall marry me!" he cried. "Your face is as sweet as your voice!"

"I must ask my mother first," said Rosemary. So the two of them went to the cottage and much to the mother's surprise and Rosalind's envy, the prince asked for Rosemary as his wife.

What a to-do there was then! The prince said that he would come the next day to fetch Rosemary, and she should be his lovely bride. He rode off, and the maiden's mother at once began to get things ready.

"You must wear your white silk frock," she said, "and that wonderful cloak you have got. Did the prince give it to you? And how comes it that you sang so beautifully as you sat by the well?"

Then Rosemary told her mother and sister of all that had happened in the little candy house with the old witch. Rosalind listened enviously. How she wished *she* could get a glittering cloak too!

The next day Rosemary was wedded to the prince and everyone said what a beautiful bride she was. Rosalind frowned and pouted when she saw her sister made a princess. *She* meant to be one as well.

"I shall go to the candy house and get a cloak like Rosemary's," she said to herself. "Then I shall marry a prince too."

So the next day she set off through the wood and very soon came to the little candy house. Her walk had made her hungry and she began to pick tarts and cakes off the wall as fast as she could.

"What are you doing, what are you doing!" screamed the old witch, suddenly running out of the door. "You naughty girl, pulling my house to pieces like that."

"Don't get into such a temper," said Rosalind. "I'll bake for you to-morrow, if you'll let me spend the night here."

The old dame remembered how well the other girl had worked, and she bade Rosalind enter.

"You must be up early if you are going to bake,"

As she sang, who should ride up but the prince of the land!

she said. "So do not oversleep. You may rest on that bed by the fire."

Rosalind slept soundly. She woke early, but she was so warm and comfortable that she did not want to get up and work. "Let the old woman get up first," she said to herself. "I am her guest—she should bring me my breakfast!" So the lazy girl lay there and did nothing. The old dame awoke and was disappointed to find that this girl did not bring her any tea. She got up and went into the kitchen. There was Rosalind, lying yawning.

"You lazy maid!" scolded the old witch. "Didn't I say you were to get up early and bake? Rouse yourself quickly."

Rosalind was afraid and got up quickly. The old woman made a pot of tea and some buttery toast, but she did not offer any to Rosalind.

"When you have baked, then you shall eat," she said. The maiden sulked and said nothing. She got ready the baking things, and made up the fire.

Rosalind was not good at making cakes and pies. She had so often made Rosemary do them for her that she did not properly know the way. So she did very badly. Her tarts were all burnt and her cakes were black. The witch was very angry.

"So this is the way you wasted my good flour and butter!" she scolded. "You lazy girl, any-one can see you have never taken the trouble to learn your work properly. Leave my cottage at once, or I will certainly beat you."

"You gave my sister a brooch and a cloak," said Rosalind, sulkily. "Aren't you going to treat me the same?"

The witch looked at Rosalind slyly.

"Very well," she said. "You shall have the same choice as your sister—though you are as different from that merry-hearted maid as chalk is from cheese!"

She pulled the box of brooches from the drawer, and bade Rosalind choose one. The greedy girl took the one she thought the richest—a little frog in pure gold. She pinned it to her frock, and asked for her cloak.

"Choose!" said the witch, and took her to where the cloaks hung in a row, only the linings showing. Rosalind picked one with a golden lining and put it over her shoulder. Now indeed she would look beautiful and would marry a prince!

Without saying a word of thanks, she ran out of the cottage and went towards her home. She heard the witch laughing loudly as she shut the door of the candy house, but she did not know why.

Alas for Rosalind! Although her cloak had a golden lining, the outer side was all moth-eaten and worn. Even as she walked home the cloak fell into holes, and soon she saw that it was no better than rags. How angry she was!

"Where have you been, you naughty girl?" cried her mother when she saw her.

"I shan't tell you," answered Rosalind rudely and ran out to the well, crying. Then she remembered how Rosemary had sung so sweetly there, and she opened her mouth to sing too.

But alas! She had chosen a frog for her brooch and she could only croak dismally. People gathered round her and laughed. Then up galloped a horseman, a brother of the prince who had married Rosemary. He had heard that Rosemary had a sister, and he thought that if she were one half so sweet as his brother's bride, he could not do better than marry her.

But when he saw the sulky girl in her ragged cloak, croaking dolefully by the well, he turned his horse's head homewards and galloped away again. This was no bride for him!

As she saw the prince vanish from sight, the unhappy girl burst into tears and, throwing away her cloak and brooch, ran sobbing to her mother.

"Now that Rosemary has gone, you will have to work hard," said her mother. "Come, set the fire going and we will do the washing!"

So while merry, kind-hearted Rosemary sat by her prince and smiled, sulky Rosalind had to do all the work in her mother's cottage—and soon she grew into a hard-working, sensible maid, and married a farmer's son nearby. But never, never, did she tell him of her visit to the little candy house!

The Peasant Boy and the Prince

THERE was once a little peasant boy who lived with his mother, father, and baby sister. He got up early every day and milked the cow, and after breakfast he went to the village school with all the other children. He did odd jobs for his father, and ran errands for his mother, and altogether had a very happy life.

But he thought he was dreadfully unhappy, and he was always complaining because he hadn't been born a prince.

"If I were a prince, I would have everything I liked to eat and drink, and I needn't run errands, nor milk the cow," he grumbled. "I would have a pony of my own, and servants to wait on me, and everyone would bow down to me."

"Don't talk nonsense," said his mother. "You're happier as you are."

But Rollo didn't think so. He was always longing to be a prince. And then one day he got his chance!

It happened like this. He was trudging along through the wood on his way home from school, when he suddenly saw a small boy on a pony come tearing past him. Rollo jumped aside in a hurry, and the other boy reined in.

"I'm so sorry!" he called. "I didn't mean to give you a fright, but my pony was stung by a fly, and suddenly galloped off."

Rollo looked up at the boy who was speaking. Then he stared hard. The other boy stared back.

"Good gracious me!" cried Rollo. "Why, we're exactly alike! I might be looking into a mirror and seeing myself!"

"What a queer thing!" said the other boy. "Our hair is the same, and our eyes and nose and chin and everything! Why, we might be twin brothers! Who are you?"

"I'm Rollo, son of the peasant who lives at the other side of this wood," said Rollo. "Who are you?"

"I'm Oliver, son of the King and Queen," said the boy. "But I wish I was you, I can tell you!"

"You wish you were me!" cried Rollo, in amazement. "Why, *I'd* give anything in the world to be a prince! I wish I could change places with you, I can tell you!"

Oliver laughed. Then he slipped down from his pony, and came close up to Rollo.

"Why shouldn't you change places with me, just for a little while?" he whispered. "We are so alike that no one would ever know. Come, let us change into each other's clothes, Rollo—quickly, before my tutor finds me!"

Rollo could hardly believe his ears. Change places with the prince! Could it be true? But Oliver gave him no time to think. He stripped off his fine tunic and knickerbockers, and tossed them to Rollo. Then off came his silken underclothes, and his beautiful stockings and shoes.

Rollo took off his coat and knickerbockers, which was all he wore in the summertime, and gave them to Oliver. He felt very much ashamed of them, for they were old and patched, but at least they were spotlessly clean. He had no shoes nor stockings, for he had to go barefoot in summer-time.

"Are these the only clothes you wear?" asked the prince, putting them on.

"Yes," said Rollo, in a small voice.

"My, aren't you lucky!" cried the Prince gaily. "Fancy not having to wear any shoes or stockings!"

Rollo stared at Oliver in surprise, and carefully put on all the lovely clothes that the prince had taken off. He felt very grand indeed, and his heart beat excitedly.

"Now, listen," said the prince. "You won't see much of my father and mother, the King and Queen, because they are always so busy, but remember to call them Your Majesty when you speak to them. Things are very strict at our court. You'll find that Sir Neville will be the one you see most of—he's my chief tutor—teacher, you know, and he's supposed to look after me. Then there's Lady Lucy, who's a kind of nurse—mind and be very polite to her, or she'll punish you. Now tell me about your home."

"Well, there's Mother and Father, and you call them Mother and Father," said Rollo. "And there's Bonny, my little sister, who'll want you to play with her. That's all."

"It sounds very nice," said the prince. "Fancy living all alone with your father and mother and baby sister! How very lucky you are! I live with about six hundred people, and hardly ever see my parents at all! What fun I'm going to have!"

"And what fun *I'm* going to have!" cried Rollo, suddenly thinking that at last he was going to have his wish—he was going to be a real live prince, with a pony of his own, and servants to wait on him, and everything he liked to eat and drink! How grand he would feel!

"Wait here until Sir Neville comes and finds you," said Oliver. "I'll go on to your home now. We'll meet here in a fortnight's time, and then we can change back again if either of us wants to."

"Well, I'm sure *I* shan't want to change back into a peasant boy again!" said Rollo. "I'd like to go on being a prince all my life!"

"Well, you can!" laughed Oliver, going off through the wood. "I don't want to wear shoes and stockings again, I can tell you!"

Rollo waited on the pony in great excitement. At last he heard the sound of hoofs, and saw a grey-haired, disagreeable-looking man coming along on a big horse.

He came up to Rollo and glared at him.

"How many times have I told Your Royal Highness not to gallop off alone like that?" he said sharply. "You know perfectly well that you are not allowed out of my sight. Any more nonsense of this sort, and I shall tell His Majesty the King how wicked you are."

Rollo listened to him with the greatest astonishment. Was this the way that people spoke to the prince? He felt frightened of the sharp-tongued man.

"I'm sorry," he said. "A fly stung the pony and he bolted away."

"Yes, I've heard that excuse before," said Sir Neville. "Now kindly ride with me to the palace. We shall be late for your dinner, if we are not careful, and what Lady Lucy would say to that, I really don't know."

Rollo smiled to himself. What did he care for Lady Lucy? Wasn't he the prince? He'd order her head to be cut off if she grumbled at *him*! And what would he have for dinner, he wondered. Duck and green peas? Turkey? Ice-cream? Jellies of all colours? Chocolates in dozens? Aha! He was in for a good time!

He rode along very happily, and was tremendously pleased when the people he met waved to him and shouted. He waved back to them,

25

but Sir Neville seemed very much surprised. "Have you forgotten how to salute properly?" he asked. "Don't you know that waving is forbidden to you?"

Rollo went red, and watched Sir Neville saluting the people very stiffly. He did the same, and soon found his arm beginning to ache badly. There seemed hundreds of people to salute, and Rollo became very tired of it.

At last he came in sight of the palace. It glittered in the sun, and looked simply beautiful. Rollo wondered what kind of a bedroom he would have—very grand, he expected, with golden chairs to sit on, and a golden bed to lie on. Perhaps he would eat off golden plates, too, with the King and Queen! What a lovely life!

Someone led his pony away when he dismounted inside the palace gates, and then he followed Sir Neville into the palace. He went through a vast hall, very grand indeed, with footmen standing at each side. Then up scores of stairs he climbed, and came to a white door. Through this he passed, and found himself in a sunny room with a white table in the middle and chairs around the wall.

A cross-looking lady was sitting in one of the chairs, knitting. She looked up as he came in.

"Late again!" she said. "Now go and wash your hands quickly, Your Highness, for the gong has gone for your dinner."

Rollo went to where he saw a basin fixed to the wall, and hurriedly washed his hands. He was longing to have his dinner. He finished drying himself just as a footman brought in a covered dish. He ran to the table.

"Oliver!" cried Lady Lucy. "Do you call that washing your hands? Go and wash them properly this minute!"

Rollo stared at her angrily. Did she think that was the way to speak to a prince?

"They're clean enough," he said. "I'm going to have my dinner."

"Have you lost your manners?" cried Lady Lucy, in astonishment. "You'll have no dinner until you wash your hands properly!"

"Indeed I will!" said Rollo, sitting down at the table.

"Footman, take away His Highness's dinner," said Lady Lucy.

"Leave it here," commanded Rollo. To his enormous surprise, the footman took not the slightest notice of him but at once took up the covered dish and bore it away again.

Rollo glared at Lady Lucy, and she looked back at him.

"I suppose you've got one of your naughty moods on," she said, taking up her knitting. "Very well, if you choose to go without your dinner, you can."

Rollo was angry, but he soon saw that he must do as he was told, prince or no prince. So he went and washed his hands thoroughly, with a very ill grace, and then came and sat down again. The footman put down the dish in front of him once more, and lifted the lid. Rollo stared at the contents, expecting he didn't know what—and all he saw was something that looked very like the stew his mother made for him at home, but which didn't smell half so good!

"Take this away, and bring me duck and green peas," ordered Rollo.

"Now listen to me, you naughty boy," said Lady Lucy. "If I have any more nonsense from you, you'll go straight to bed and stay there for the rest of the day."

She sounded so very fierce that Rollo said no more, but ate the stew. He thought perhaps the pudding would be something nice. But it wasn't. It was a very ordinary milk pudding, with a small baked apple to go with it. Rollo suddenly remembered that at home his mother had a treacle pudding for him, and for one minute he wished he wasn't a prince.

"I don't like this pudding," he said, in as polite a voice as he could manage. "Could I have a chocolate ice instead?"

"What next!" cried Lady Lucy. "Milk pudding is very good for you. Eat it up at once."

"I'll have your head cut off if you don't let me have what I want," said Rollo, scowling fiercely.

It was just at that moment that Sir Neville came into the room and heard Rollo's remark. He stared as if he could not believe his ears. Then with one bound, he was across the room, and dragged Rollo out of his chair.

"*What* did I hear you say?" he said, in a very stern voice. "Is *that* princely talk? Is *that* how a lady should be spoken to? Why, peasant boys have better manners! I am thoroughly ashamed of you. You will stay in this afternoon, and write out two hundred lines of 'I must remember to behave like a prince!' "

Rollo stood in the corner, and thought hard. He had supposed that he *had* been behaving like a prince—he always imagined that princes cut off people's heads if they wanted to—but now he suddenly began to see that a prince must behave *better* than other boys, not worse.

"I'm very sorry," he said to Lady Lucy. "May I have my pudding now?"

"No, you must go without," she said. "I never heard of such a thing! Threatening to have my head cut off, indeed! A fine thing if the King and Queen got to hear of your rudeness!"

The afternoon passed very tiresomely for Rollo. He sat at a desk and wrote out "I must behave like a prince" two hundred times. He hoped that tea would be nicer than dinner. But it wasn't. There was nothing but bread and butter, and a small piece of cake. Rollo thought longingly of his mother's home-made jam and hot scones.

"Your geography master wants you to sit with him for an hour after tea," said Lady Lucy, still knitting away. " Some land has been added to the kingdom, and your father the King wants you to learn about it."

Rollo was disgusted. Fancy doing lessons after tea! But he had to, and for a whole hour he sat with a dry old man who showed him on a map where a new colony had been added to the kingdom, and made him learn its name, its towns and the things it grew. How very dull it was!

Then just when he thought he really would be allowed to play, Lady Lucy said it was bedtime! Bedtime! At half-past six!

"Can't I just go and play in the garden first?" asked Rollo. "It's dreadfully early for bed."

"Well, you want to grow up a fine, healthy man, don't you?" said Lady Lucy. "If you are weak, you'll never be able to stand the hard work that a king has to do all day long—visiting hospitals and opening new buildings, attending meetings and all kinds of things! Still, you can go into the garden for ten minutes, if you like."

He went. It was just like a grand park, he thought. It wasn't like a proper garden, and there were no nice cosy corners to sit in. But there were some lovely flowers, and Rollo thought he would like some. So he began to pick a great bunch.

But up came a gardener in a great hurry, and begged His Highness not to do that, and Lady Lucy was cross with him too.

"You know quite well that that upsets the gardeners," she scolded. "Besides, if you want flowers, you can ask one of the under-gardeners to pick you some. You're not supposed to pick them yourself, as I've told you often."

Rollo went to bed rather miserable. His bedroom was an enormous room, very bare, with a large bed in the middle. There were no gold chairs as he had imagined. Everything was plain.

"Will the Queen come and kiss me good night?" he asked.

"Of course not," said Lady Lucy. "She's much too busy."

Rollo thought about his own mother, who was never too busy to tuck him up and kiss him. Then he went to sleep.

In the morning he awoke full of delight again, to think that he was a prince. But the day was most unpleasant. Breakfast was just porridge and an egg, and he wasn't allowed to have treacle as he did at home. All the morning he had to work hard with four different tutors, and Sir Neville rapped him on his knuckles if he didn't attend.

It wasn't any fun having lessons alone. Rollo missed all the boys and girls he usually went to school with. He had ten minutes' playtime in the middle of the morning, but there wasn't anyone to play with.

In the afternoon he was taken to the Council Chamber, where the King and Queen sat, and many solemn, serious men. He had to bow to the King and kiss the Queen's hand, but neither of them kissed him, or made a fuss of him, as he had expected them to.

"Why have I got to stay and listen to all this dull stuff?" he whispered to Sir Neville.

"Sh!" said Sir Neville. "All princes must attend meetings of this kind, for they learn then what is going on in their country."

All afternoon Rollo yawned and blinked. He didn't understand a word of what anyone was saying, and he was very cross when Sir Neville poked him hard to make him sit up straight. He was glad when tea-time came and he left the dull old meeting.

"Why must princes lead such a dull life?" he asked Sir Neville. "Why, I've been hard at work all day! Peasant boys have a much nicer time."

"Princes must work hard because they are the servants of their people," said Sir Neville. "When you grow up you will have to lead your people and rule them wisely and well, and so you must begin learning when you are a boy."

"But I always thought that the people were the servants of the princes!" said Rollo, in astonishment.

"What a dreadful thing to say!" cried Lady Lucy. "After all we've taught you, too! That's a very old-fashioned idea! The more people you have under you, the harder you must work to make them happy, and don't you forget that, Your Highness. Kings and queens wish they were just ordinary people, who could live in dear little houses with dear little gardens, and have their children all to themselves, and nothing to bother about except shopping and housework and gardening. But they must do their duty as kings and queens, and work harder than anyone."

Rollo listened, and his heart sank. He didn't want to be a prince after all. It wasn't any fun. Princes hadn't got proper fathers and mothers, and he couldn't get dirty or fight with other boys, and all the day there were lessons by himself, and

Sir Neville and Lady Lucy were always following him about to see that he was good and princely.

Rollo wanted his mother. He wanted his baby sister to play with. He longed to taste his mother's cakes again. He wished he could milk old Buttercup the cow. He wondered what his school friends were doing. In fact, he was dreadfully homesick.

That night, when he was all alone in his big bedroom, Rollo got up and dressed himself. He stole out of the palace, and made his way to the little stable where the pony was kept. He jumped on its back, galloped past the astonished sentry at the gate, and turned towards home.

He came to his little cottage, and jumped off the pony. Quickly he climbed up the pear tree that stood by his own little bedroom window, and dropped into the room.

Oliver was lying asleep in his bed with a happy smile on his lips. By his side was a fine new whistle, made by Rollo's father. Rollo shook Oliver awake. He sat up and looked in astonishment at Rollo.

"Look here," he said. "The fortnight isn't up. Go back."

"I can't," said Rollo. "I hate being a prince, always being with some tutor or other, never being free and alone, and having to attend dull old councils, and never having a mother to kiss me at night, and oh, lots of other things. I want to be Rollo again, and have my own mother and father and baby sister."

"But *I* don't want to go back yet," said Oliver. "I don't ever want to go back. Why, it's lovely here, Rollo. Your mother's a darling, and my, can't she cook! I love going to school with other children, too; we have such jolly games. And your baby sister is the dearest little thing. I don't have to work nearly so hard, either. All I have to do is to milk that nice old cow, and go errands for your mother. There's plenty of time to play. Please stay and be prince instead of me."

But Rollo wouldn't.

"I should make a very bad king," he said. "You will make a good one, so for the sake of your people, you ought to go back, Oliver."

Oliver grunted and groaned, but he got up and dressed in his right clothes. Rollo slipped into his own little bed, and felt happier than he had ever been in his life before.

"Well, good-bye," said Oliver, getting out of the window. "I've had a perfectly lovely time. You're the luckiest boy in the world, Rollo, and don't you forget it."

When Rollo woke in the morning, he rushed into his mother's room. He felt as if he must hug his mother and father and kiss his baby sister before he did anything else.

"Why, Rollo!" said his mother laughing at his happy face. "You look as happy as a prince!"

"Oh, no, Mother," said Rollo. "Princes aren't nearly as happy as I am! I know that for certain sure! I'd rather be me than any prince in the land!"

Benny and the Princess

BENNY was a little boy tramp. He had no home, no mother and no father. He went about the world doing odd jobs here and there, earning a penny one day, twopence the next, and maybe nothing the day after.

He was often very lonely. He sometimes looked into windows at night-time when the lamps were lit, and wished he had a cosy home where there was someone who loved him.

"Never mind!" he said to himself. "One day I'll find someone who loves me, and then I can love them back, and we'll have a nice little home together."

One week, Benny found it very hard to get work. Nobody seemed to want any jobs done at all. There were no gardens that needed digging, no wood that wanted chopping, and no horses that wanted holding. Benny was very hungry, and wondered what he could do.

Then he suddenly saw a big notice by the side of the road. This is what it said:

DANGER. BEWARE OF GIANTS.

"That's funny," said Benny. "Fancy there being any giants about here!"

He looked round, but he couldn't see any. Then he spied a carter coming slowly towards him, with a load of sacks of potatoes. He hailed him, and asked for a lift.

"You'd better not come with me," said the carter. "I've got to deliver these potatoes a bit too near the giants' castle, for my liking!"

"I'm not afraid!" said Benny. "Let me come, do, for I'm tired."

"Jump up, then," said the carter.

So up Benny sprang, and sat in the cart. He began to ask the carter questions about the giants, and the man told him all he wanted to know.

"There's a giants' castle over yonder," he said, pointing with his whip to the west. "Two great giants live in it, and it is said that they take people prisoner when they can, and hold them to ransom. I heard they were wanting another servant, but you can guess nobody is likely to go there!"

"Dear me!" said Benny. "I wonder if they would take *me* for their servant. Do you think they would?"

"What! Do you mean to say you'd go to live with great ugly giants?" cried the carter in amazement. "You keep away from them, my boy, or maybe they'll have you for dinner."

Benny thought about it for a while, and then he made up his mind. He would try to get a job in the giants' castle. That would be better than starving, anyway, and if he thought the giants were likely to eat him he would run away.

"You'd better come back with me on my cart," said the carter, when he had delivered his sacks at a little house by the roadside. "If you get down here, you'll meet the giants, perhaps."

"That's just what I want to do!" said Benny. He leapt down, thanked the surprised carter, and ran down the road. It wound up a hill, and when he came to the top he saw the giants' castle in the distance.

The sun was setting as he came near it, and the windows glistened and shone.

He walked boldly up to the back door, which was about twenty times as high as he was, and pulled hard at the bell.

The door opened, and a giant servant peered out. He didn't see Benny, who only came about as high as his knee, so he shut the door again. The boy pulled the bell hard, and once more the giant peered round the door, looking very much surprised.

"Hi!" called Benny. "Look down, not up! Can't you see me?"

The giant looked down in surprise. When he saw Benny he grinned broadly.

"Jumping pigs!" he said. "What a little mannikin! What may you want, shrimp?"

"I hear the giants want a servant," said Benny. "Will I do?"

The giant roared with laughter.

"You!" he said. "Why, what could *you* do?"

"Anything!" said Benny, stepping inside. "Just go and tell the giants I am here, will you?"

The servant gaped at Benny's order, but he turned and trotted off, making a noise like thunder on the wooden floor. Soon he came back again.

"The masters want to see you," he said. So Benny followed him, looking as bold and brave as could be, but inside he was feeling very trembly indeed.

The two giants who wanted to see him were simply enormous. Their servant seemed quite a dwarf beside them. They picked Benny up, and stood him on a table, looking at him very closely.

"He seems a smart lad," said one of them in a great booming voice.

"He is neat and clean, too," said the other. Then he spoke to Benny.

"We have a little guest with us," he said, with a grin that showed all his big teeth. "She is not eating very well, and we think that our own servant is too clumsy to prepare her meals as she likes them. We want a smaller servant who will please her better. Can you cook, prepare dainty meals, and generally make yourself useful to our guest?"

"Certainly," said Benny, thinking that the giants had a little niece staying with them. "I will do my best."

So the giants engaged him, and he was told to start on his duties the very next day.

Next morning he prepared a nice breakfast, set it on the smallest tray he could find, and then followed the giant servant to the top of the castle. The servant unlocked a heavy door, and flung it open. Benny went in, carrying his tray carefully.

And then he got such a surprise! For the guest was no niece of the giants, but a lovely little Princess, who was being kept a prisoner by them. He nearly dropped the tray when he saw her.

"Why!" he cried. "You are no giant! You are a Princess! Where do you come from, and how long have you been here?"

"Silence!" shouted the giant servant, pulling Benny's ear and nearly deafening him. "The masters say that you and the Princess must not speak a word to one another!"

Benny said no more. The Princess said never a word in reply, for she was afraid of getting Benny into trouble. But she managed to give him one or two looks, which told him as plainly as could be that she was unhappy and wanted to escape.

Benny followed the giant servant downstairs, thinking very hard. He thought the little Princess was the loveliest thing he had ever seen. Every time he remembered her sweet face a little warm feeling crept round his heart, so he knew that

39

he had found someone to love, and he was very happy.

"Now, how can I rescue her?" he wondered. "I must certainly get her away from here!"

"If you think you're going to speak to the Princess or send messages to her, you can get the idea out of your head!" said the giant servant when they were downstairs again. "I have orders to prevent anything of the sort."

Benny said nothing for he did not want to anger the servant. Instead, he began to think out delicious meals for the Princess. He made a small tray, and looked for the very tiniest dishes and plates in the castle, for he knew the Princess would not like her meals set on dishes as large as tables.

Then he began to think how he might get her away in safety. First of all, how was he to tell her things? He soon thought of a way.

"I'll write my messages on strips of paper," he said. "Then I'll make some cakes, and put the paper round them. Both paper and cake will be baked together, which, as anybody knows, is the right way to bake, and then the princess can read my messages in secret! Now how can I tell her what I am going to do?"

That night he made himself a bow and a few arrows. He slipped out into the moonlight and looked for the Princess's window. He soon saw it, for she sat by a lamp sewing, and he could see her golden head, bent over her needle.

He wrote a note, and stuck it on the end of an arrow. Then he shot it up at her window. It just missed it, and fell back again. He shot another, with a second note on it. This time it struck the side of the window, and made a noise. The Princess heard it and raised her head.

Benny shot a third arrow. It flew right in at the window, and landed at the feet of the startled girl. She picked it up and saw the note.

"This is to tell you that I mean to rescue you," she read. "Please tear off the paper you will find round the cakes I bake for you, and you will see my messages written there. Shooting letters with arrows is too dangerous. Take heart, Princess, for I will be your knight.

"BENNY"

How glad the Princess was! She ran to the window, and waved her hand in the moonlight. Benny knew that she had read his message, and was content.

Every day he baked her a little cake, and wrote his message on the paper round it. The giant servant used to take a skewer, and poke it through the cake, to see if Benny had put notes inside— but it never came into his head that the boy had been clever enough to write his messages on the paper baked round the cake itself. So he didn't find out the secret.

Benny tried hard to think of some way of escape. It was very difficult, for the two giants always seemed to be about, and as for the giant servant, he never let Benny out of his sight.

Then, one very hot day, Benny's chance came. He heard the sound of carriage wheels, and popped his head out of the window. To his joy he saw that the two giants were in it driving away from the castle.

"That's got rid of two, anyway!" he said. "Now what about the servant? Ah, I've got an idea! If only it will work!"

"Where have our masters gone?" he asked the servant. "Will they be long?"

"About six hours," said the giant, with a yawn.

"Then don't let's do any work this afternoon," said Benny. "Let's go to sleep."

"No," said the giant, suspiciously. "You'll run off, if I so much as shut my eyes, I know!"

"Well, *I'll* do some work, and you just have a nice rest," said Benny. "You'll be able to hear me working, so you'll know I'm here all right. I'll wash and scrub the kitchen floor."

"Very well," said the giant. "I'll put my chair right in the middle, then you won't need to disturb me."

He put his easy chair right in the middle of the vast kitchen, and sat down. Benny got out a pail and cloth, and began to wash the floor. He watched the giant carefully, and soon saw that what he hoped would happen, was happening. The giant was falling asleep.

Then Benny ran to the cupboard, and got out the polish and a duster. He had an idea. He began to polish the wooden floor of the kitchen as if his life depended on it. The giant occasionally opened his eyes but, seeing Benny busy, shut them again at once. The youth went on with his work, until he had made all the floor shiny and slippery. Then he began to polish the long passage that led out of the kitchen to the hall. The giant heard him, and fell asleep for the sixth time.

When Benny had finished, he crawled on his knees to the snoring giant. He carefully picked the key of the tower-room from the giant's belt, and then began to crawl back again. The giant awoke, opened his eyes, and looked for Benny. At once the boy began to rub his duster on the floor, as if he were still cleaning it. The giant shut his eyes, and began to snore once more.

Benny took his chance. He tore up the stairs to the tower-room, unlocked it, and ran to the Princess. He took her hand, and begged her to come with him.

"The two giants are out," he said. "As for the servant, he is asleep—but if he awakes, and tries to come after us, he will find it difficult to get out of the kitchen—for I have polished the floor so highly that he will find it impossible to walk across it!"

The Princess held his hand, and together they ran down the stairs. They crept out of the front door, and tiptoed down the steps, afraid of making a noise in case they awakened the giant. But alas! He awoke just at that moment, and heard them!

"Benny!" he called. "BENNY! Where are you? Come here at once!"

When no Benny came, the giant leapt to his feet and tried to run across the floor—but it was so terribly slippery that he fell on his nose at once! He tried to get up, but he couldn't, for the floor was as slippery as ice. He slid here, and slipped there, and at last managed to stand up again.

Then plonk! Down he went once more. It would have been a funny sight to watch if anyone had been there to see. He scrambled and slipped, and slipped and scrambled, and at last got to the door. But then there was the long slippery passage to go down!

The servant gave it up at last. He was so tired of bumping his nose, his knees, and his elbows. He simply sat down on the floor and waited.

Soon the two giants came home. They walked to the kitchen to speak to their servant—and crash! Down they both went on the polished floor! They clutched at one another, and slid all over the place, getting mixed up with the surprised servant. At last they all sat still and looked at one another.

"What do you mean by this?" asked the giants, scowling at the servant. "This is a fine thing to do to the floor."

"It's not my fault," said the servant, sulkily. "Benny did it, and now he's gone, and I don't know where he is. He's taken the key of the tower-room too, so I expect the Princess is escaping with him."

"Good gracious!" cried the giants, and tried to leap to their feet. But down they went again, and slithered all along the passage. By the time they managed to get to the front door and start chasing Benny and the Princess, it was too late.

Benny was far away. He and the Princess had run for miles. They had passed the notice-board that said: "Beware of Giants," and were hurrying to the east. Soon they saw a fine carriage rolling along the road, and Benny sprang out to stop it.

"Ho, ho! What's this!" cried the coachman, flicking at Benny with his whip. "How dare you stop the carriage of the Lord High Chamberlain?"

"Oh!" squeaked the Princess in delight. "He's my uncle!"

A bearded face appeared at the window, and then the door was flung open.

"Princess! My dear little long-lost niece!" cried the Chamberlain. "How did you come here? We have lost you for months, and looked for you everywhere!"

The Princess hugged him, and begged to be taken to her parents, the King and Queen. Off rolled the carriage once more, with the Chamberlain, the Princess, and Benny sitting inside.

It was not long before they arrived at the palace. How glad the King and Queen were to see their little daughter once again! They hugged and kissed her, and shook Benny's hand a hundred times.

"You shall have as much gold as you please, and I will make you a noble lord!" cried the King. "I can never be grateful to you enough."

"And I'll marry you when I'm old enough," the

45

Princess whispered in his ear, "because I love you very much, Benny."

So Benny took his gold, and became Sir Benjamin Braveheart. And people do say that next year he is going to marry the Princess, and I shouldn't be at all surprised if it is true!

The Hen, the Tray, and the Poker

THERE was once a youth who worked for a farmer in the country. This farmer had three daughters, the youngest of which was the prettiest maid anyone could wish to see. Will, the farmer's boy, fell in love with her and wanted to marry her.

But the farmer was angry when he knew this. "How dare you seek to marry my daughter!" he shouted in a fine rage. "Why, you earn but a shilling a week—you cannot keep a wife on that!"

"Well, sir," said the youth, "I work hard for you, and I am honest and strong. Cannot you give me more wages? Then I could marry your daughter and keep her in comfort."

The farmer was a mean man, and when he heard what the youth said, he laughed.

"You are not worth any more than I pay you,"

47

he said. "As for my daughter, she is not for you. She shall marry a rich man."

When the youth knew that he could not hope for more money, he took up his few belongings, wrapped them in a blue handkerchief and bade the mean farmer good-bye.

"I will go elsewhere," he said. "Mayhap I shall come to a master who will pay me well."

He set off down the lane—but the farmer's daughter ran after him with tears in her eyes, begging him not to go.

"I will come back," promised Will. "I will become rich and then I will return and marry you."

He went on his way and after two days' walking he came to a little town. In the middle of the town was an open shop and a carpenter was working busily at a bench, hammering, sawing and planing. He worked so fast that Will stayed to watch him.

As he stood there a man came up and spoke to the carpenter.

"Can you make me four chairs by Friday?" he asked. "My wife is giving a party and we want more seats."

"Sorry, sir, but I am too busy," said the carpenter in dismay. "I have a table to make, a cupboard, two windows and a door. I shall have no time to make chairs."

Then Will stepped nearer and spoke to him.

"Take me as your helper," he said. "I am quick with my hands, and I know how to make chairs and tables. I will work well, Master, and you will not be sorry."

"Very well," said the carpenter, looking Will up and down. "Can you start now? If you can, we shall be able to get the chairs done by Friday. But mind—I cannot pay you much, for I am not a rich man. Work for me for a year and a day, and in return I will give you food and a bed, and something at the end of the year."

"Done!" said Will, making up his mind to work so hard that his master would give him a large sum of money at the year's end.

So he entered the service of the carpenter and was very happy with him. He worked hard, and his master was pleased with him. At the end of the year Will went to him.

"The year and the day are ended," he said. "Do you want me any more, Master?"

"I should dearly like to keep you longer," said the carpenter, "but my own son is now old enough to help me, and must set to work to learn my trade. You have worked well, Will. Here is a gift for you."

So saying, the little carpenter went to a cupboard, unlocked the door and took out a finely carved wooden tray. Will looked at it in surprise.

"You may well look," said the carpenter. "This tray is a marvellous thing. Whenever you say to it, 'Tray, I want my breakfast,' or 'Tray, I want my dinner,' it will at once become full of good things to eat. It will be worth a fortune to you."

"Thank you, Master," said Will, gratefully. He shook hands with the kind carpenter and then set out for the farm where lived the maiden he meant to marry.

"Surely now that I have this wonderful tray which will soon make me rich, the farmer will let me marry his daughter," thought Will.

He walked on till night fell, and then came to a cottage by the roadside. He knocked at the door and asked if he might have shelter for the night. A man bade him come in, and Will entered the tiny cottage.

There were two rough-looking men there, sitting over a tiny fire. Will did not like the look of them, but since there was nowhere else that he could go for the night he made up his mind to stop there.

"We can give you a bed of straw by the fire," said one of the men. "But we can only let you have a crust of bread for supper. There is nothing else in the house."

"Oh, I will provide supper!" said Will. He set his wooden tray on the table and spoke to it commandingly.

"Tray, I want my supper!" he said. At once the tray became covered with six dishes. There were sausages, potatoes, cabbage, treacle pudding, cheese and a bowl of grapes. How the two men stared to see such a marvellous sight!

Will took all the things off the tray and put them on the table. Then once more he said, "Tray, I want my supper!" For the second time the tray became covered with dishes, and Will put them on the table. Then he spoke to the tray again, and another fine supper appeared. Now there was a meal for each of them, and they all fell to with a good appetite.

Afterwards Will was sleepy and he lay down by the fire. He soon fell fast asleep. When the two men saw this they began to whisper together and point to the tray. One of them had been a carpenter, and after a while he took the tray and slipped out of the room. In two hours he came back with a tray so like the first that it was difficult to tell the difference. He had made this to put in place of the first, which the two men meant to keep and use for themselves.

In the morning Will woke up early, and without waiting for breakfast he took up the tray where it lay on the table and walked off. All day he travelled, and at last when dusk was falling came to the farm.

He walked boldly into the house and spoke to the farmer.

"I come to claim your daughter," he said.

"Why, are you rich?" asked the farmer, mockingly.

"No," said Will, "but I have a wonderful tray here that will soon make my fortune. I have only to command it and it will at once provide me with breakfast, dinner or supper."

"Let us see this marvel," said the farmer, and he and his three daughters gathered round the tray.

"Tray, I want my supper!" said Will. The tray lay on the table and did nothing. Will was surprised. He spoke again more loudly.

"Tray, I want my supper!" he said. But still the tray did nothing at all—and indeed, how could it? It was nothing but an ordinary wooden one.

Then the farmer was very angry. He caught up his stick and chased Will out of the house, though his youngest daughter wept and cried bitterly. Poor Will ran far away, grieved and puzzled to think that his tray had so soon lost its magic.

He slept the night in a ditch, and the next day journeyed on to find work. But no matter where he begged for work, he could get none. All that day and the next he tramped hard, and at last, when night fell, he came to a small cottage. There was a pump at the bottom of the garden and a little old woman was pumping there. She was out of breath and panting.

"Let me do that for you!" said Will. "It is too hard for you, old dame."

"Now that is very kind of you," said the old woman, gratefully. "Pump me two buckets full, please, and carry them to the house."

Will did so, and the old woman looked at his bright face.

"You're a likely lad!" she said. "How I wish I had you to work for me until my own boy comes home from foreign lands. There's too much for me to do here."

"Well, dame, I'd be glad to be your servant," said Will at once. "I want work and it is difficult to get. I will start right away."

"Work for me till my boy comes home," said the dame. "I'll give you good food and a comfortable bed, and something for yourself at the end of the time."

So Will became the servant of the little old woman. He pumped the water, scrubbed the floors, dug the garden, mended the windows, picked the fruit and did everything he could. Only one thing he was not allowed to do, and that was to feed the old dame's hens. This she always did herself every morning and evening.

When Will had worked for nine months, the old woman's boy came home again, and she said that she would no longer have room for Will.

"You have worked well and willingly," she said. "Here is something for yourself. It should make your fortune for you."

She handed him a little red hen that clucked loudly. Will was surprised and wondered how a hen could make his fortune.

"Pull her tail gently and she will lay an egg for you," said the old dame. "Her eggs are always half-silver and half-gold. You will be able to make much money from her."

Will thanked the old woman very much and set out once more, the little red hen tucked under his arm. He walked until night-time and then found himself in a thick wood. He could see no house anywhere, but as he walked through the trees he saw the light of a fire. He walked towards it, and who should he see sitting by the fire but the two men in whose cottage he had once spent the night!

"Hallo, my boy!" said one of the men, seeing at a glance that it was the same youth as before.

"Have you lost your way? Spend the night by our fire. We have the remains of a good supper here which you can have."

Will was very grateful. He ate the supper they gave him, and then wondered how he should pay for it, for he had no money. He thought of his little red hen, and taking it under his arm he went a little way away where the two men could not see him.

"Hen, lay an egg!" he said, and pulled the bird's tail gently. At once the little thing clucked loudly and laid a small egg, half-silver and half-gold. Will picked it up and looked at it.

"Now my fortune is indeed made!" he thought.

One of the two men had crept after him and had hidden behind a tree to watch what he was going to do. When he saw what the hen did, he ran back to his companion and told him what he had seen. Then Will returned and gave the egg to them, saying that it was in payment for his supper. After that he lay down by the fire and fell fast asleep.

In the night the two men went to a nearby farm, and stole a little red hen from the hen-shed. They came back to the wood and put it in the place of Will's red hen. Then they took Will's bird to their cottage, some miles away.

The youth awoke in the morning and looked round for his hen. There it was, tied to a bough not far off, where he had put it the night before. But the two men were gone. Will was surprised, but he thought little of it. He tucked the hen under his arm and set off towards the farm where his sweetheart lived.

He arrived there in the evening and strode into the kitchen where the farmer and his daughters sat at supper.

"How now!" cried the farmer in a rage. "Here you are back again, like a bad penny! Do you mean to tell me you are rich?"

"Yes," said Will. "I have here a little red hen which will make my fortune; for every time I pull her tail she lays me an egg, half-silver and half-gold."

He set the hen on a table, and the farmer and his family came round. Will pulled the bird's tail gently, and commanded it to lay him an egg. But alas! The hen did nothing. How could it, when it was but an ordinary bird?

Will was full of dismay. Surely the magic was not gone from the hen already! He pulled its tail again, harder this time—but the hen simply clucked, and did nothing.

"You have deceived us again!" cried the farmer in a rage, and he picked up his stick. Will did not wait to be beaten, but fled away as fast as his legs could carry him, disappointed and sad.

He wandered on and on until at last he came to a blacksmith's. The smith was working in his forge. Will stood and watched him. The smith saw him standing there, and spoke to him.

"Well, lad," he said, "you look a good strong fellow. Would you like to work with me for a year and a day? I need someone to help me."

"Willingly," said Will, gladly. He took off his coat and set to work at once. He was very strong and he liked working with the smith. All kinds of things they made, from horseshoes to plough-shares, and all day long the great fire roared.

At the end of a year and a day the smith clapped Will on the back and said that if he chose he could stay with him and share his business, for the lad had worked well.

"Thank you, Master," said Will. "But first grant me a holiday so that I may go and see the pretty maiden I love."

"You may have three days," said the smith. "And wait! I have something for you!"

He went to the back of the smithy and took down from the shelf an old black poker.

"Take this," he said to Will. "It will be useful to you. If you have an enemy you have only to say, 'Now, poker, go for him!' and the poker will beat your foe till he begs for mercy."

Will took the poker and thanked the smith. Then he set off once more for the farm. On the way he came to the cottage where he had once spent the night with the two wicked men. Will had often thought about his tray and his little red hen, and he now felt sure that the two men had exchanged them for others of no use. He meant to get them back if he could. So he knocked loudly at the cottage door.

One of the men came to the door, and when he saw that it was Will, he opened the door wide and bade the youth enter. Will strode inside and

Will fled away as fast as his legs could carry him.

asked if he might have a night's shelter again.

"You are very welcome," said the two men, and they looked at Will to see what wonderful thing he had with him this time. But all he had was an old black poker.

The two men eyed it, and wondered what magic it contained. Will did not put it down, but kept it by him all the time, and the men felt sure that it was very valuable. They made up their minds to steal it that night when Will was asleep.

As soon as the youth lay down in front of the fire, his poker by him, the men waited for him to sleep. Will was wide awake, but he pretended to snore. When they heard the snoring the men crept up to him. One of them put his hand out to take the poker—and at that moment Will sat up and cried in a loud voice:

"Now, poker, go for them!"

In a trice the black poker stood up and flew at the two astonished men. And what a drubbing it gave them! It smote them on the back and front, on the hands and legs and on the head. How they shouted and yelled, how they groaned and cried!

"Stop your poker, stop it!" they shouted to Will, who was thoroughly enjoying himself. But Will would not bid the poker stop. At last the men fell on their knees and begged him for mercy.

"I will tell the poker to stop when you tell me what you have done with my magic tray and little red hen," said Will. "I know quite well that you stole them from me and put useless ones in their place."

At first the men vowed that they knew nothing of the hen and the tray—but the poker beat them so hard that at last they confessed.

"The tray is in that cupboard over there," groaned one man.

"And the hen is out in the yard at the back," groaned the other.

"Fetch them," said Will. So one man went to get the tray and the other went outside to get the hen. The poker flew from one to the other, and would not cease its strokes. When the tray and the hen were in Will's hands, he commanded the poker to stop.

"Enough, poker," he said. "Come to me."

At once the poker flew to his hand, and stayed there quite still. Then Will left the cottage with his tray, hen and poker, and walked steadily through the night. At daybreak he came to the farm, and he waited until he saw smoke rising from the kitchen chimney. Then he went to the door.

The family were sitting at breakfast. Will walked into the room, laid his tray on a chair, and said: "Tray, I want my breakfast!"

Instantly the tray became covered with a most delicious meal—bacon and eggs, coffee, toast and marmalade. The farmer and his daughters stared in amazement. Then Will set his little red hen down on the floor and spoke to it.

"Hen, lay an egg!" he said, and pulled the bird's tail gently. At once the little hen laid an egg, half-silver and half-gold. Will handed it to the farmer who stared at it as if he could not believe his eyes.

"I shall soon be rich," said Will. "Will you let me marry your daughter now? I have also a third magic thing—a poker that beats those who offend me—but *that* I will not set to work until I must."

The farmer looked at the black poker, and decided that he had better let his daughter marry this bold youth. Besides he would certainly make his fortune with the magic tray and the little red hen. So he gave his consent, and Will was overjoyed.

The maiden was married to Will that very same day. She packed up all her belongings, and two days later she went with Will to the blacksmith, who was very pleased to see them.

Will became a fine smith, and what with the tray to provide fine meals and the hen to give him silver and gold, he soon became rich enough to build a pretty little cottage for his wife. Then indeed they were happy, and the little house was filled with singing and laughter all the day long.

As for the two wicked men they ran away and were never heard of again, which was just as well for everybody.

The Runaway Teddy Bear

ONE DAY Peter went to see his cousin Betty. She was sitting in the garden nursing a big teddy bear.

"What a fine teddy!" said Peter. "Is he yours?" "Yes, I had him for my birthday," said Betty, hugging him close. "But if I'm not careful he runs away!"

"Runs away!" said Peter, in surprise. "But how can he, Betty? He's not real."

"He's just as real as a teddy bear *can* be," said Betty. "And it's quite true, Peter. He *does* run away. He doesn't like being with anybody but me. When I lent him to Pamela, over the road, he ran away as fast as anything!"

"Where did he run to?" asked Peter.

"Not very far," said Betty, "because I saw him

going, and caught him before he was out of sight. But I'm always afraid that he'll go right away one day, and then I'll never find him again. And that would make me very sad, because I do love him so."

Just at that moment Betty's mother called her indoors.

"Betty, Betty!" she cried. "Your new shoes have just arrived, and I want you to try them on."

"I shan't be a minute," said Betty. She popped her teddy down on the chair she had been sitting in, and ran off.

Peter looked at the bear, and the bear looked back at Peter.

"I don't believe that story of Betty's about the teddy running away," thought Peter. "Whoever heard of bears going off like that?"

The bear still stared at Peter. The little boy got up, and went towards Betty's chair. The bear looked alarmed, and for a moment Peter thought he trembled.

"That's nonsense!" he said to himself. "It's only a toy teddy! I'll pick him up and cuddle him till Betty comes back. He looks lovely and cuddly."

He picked up the teddy bear, and gave him a good hug. All at once he felt the bear kick out, and begin to struggle in his arms.

"Oh! Oh! Let me go!" he cried in a voice just like his growl, very deep and grunty.

In surprise and alarm Peter let go. The bear dropped from his arms bounced on the ground and then jumped to his feet. In a trice he was running away as fast as he could go. Peter watched him in the greatest astonishment.

Then suddenly he began to think of Betty.

"Oh dear! Whatever will she say when she finds her teddy gone?" he said. "I must try to catch him!"

Off he went after the bear. The little brown animal could run very fast, and he was racing down the garden like the wind. Peter tore after him, calling loudly:

"Hie! Hie! Teddy bear, stop! Betty wants you! Hie! Hie!"

But the bear didn't stop. On he went and on. He reached the end of the garden, and ran through the little gate that led on to the lane. Peter followed after, puffing and panting. Down the lane went the bear, and over the stile that led to Breezy Hill. Then up the hill he raced as fast as he could go.

Over the stile went Peter, and up the hill too. He was gaining on the bear, and he thought that surely he would soon catch him.

Suddenly the teddy dived under a blackberry bush and disappeared. Peter forced his way underneath too, and could find no sign of the bear at all. But he found something very curious.

Let into the hillside, well hidden by the blackberry bush, was a small yellow door. There was a handle on it, very brightly polished.

"He must have gone in there!" said Peter to himself. "Well, I'll go too!"

He turned the bright handle, and opened the

door. Inside was a tiny room, and sitting at a table in the middle was an old brownie, pouring himself out a cup of strong tea.

"Well really!" he said, in a very cross voice, as Peter came in. "First a bear bursts in, and now you. And neither of you has the good manners to knock!"

"Oh, I'm very sorry!" said Peter, so full of astonishment to see a real live brownie that he hardly knew what he was saying. "Oh really, I'm very sorry. But that bear belongs to my cousin Betty, and he has run away. Do you know where he went to? He doesn't seem to be anywhere here."

"He's gone out of my back door," said the brownie, putting a large lump of sugar into his cup. "If you go after him you'll probably see him catch the green train that goes to Toyland."

"Is there a railway anywhere near here?" asked Peter in amazement. "I thought we were six miles from the nearest railway. That's what my Mother always told me, and she generally knows everything."

"Well, she's wrong this time," said the brownie. "You go through that door at the back there, and follow the passage till you come to the railway line. That's where you'll find the bear."

Peter thanked him, and pushed open a little door at the back of the room. It led on to a narrow passage, very winding, and lighted by a row of glow-worms hanging in little lamps from the roof. Peter ran down the passage, and came at last to what he thought must be a railway line—but it looked so small and narrow that he wondered what kind of train could run on such tiny lines.

Just at that moment a train came puffing up. It was very small indeed, not much bigger than Peter's big wooden engine at home. All the carriages were open trucks. Peter looked round for the bear. He must be somewhere near, and he wanted to catch him before he got on to the train.

The engine gave a funny little whistle, and stopped with such a jolt that all the passengers inside the trucks were nearly thrown out. Peter didn't get in, because he couldn't see the bear and he didn't want to go off in a train without him. The engine gave another funny little whistle, and started off again. It had not gone more than a few yards when Peter saw the teddy bear come out from a corner and throw himself into a truck.

"Bother!" cried the little boy. "He's gone after all! *Now* what am I to do?"

He started to run after the train, and shouted loudly. A sandy rabbit who was in the last truck, heard him, and waved to him excitedly to come on. Peter ran along the line as fast as he could, and to his delight he saw the train stopping at a signal that was against it. He got up to the last truck just in time, climbed in as the signal arm moved, and the train went on again.

"A near squeak," said the sandy rabbit, putting on an enormous pair of glasses, and looking at Peter through them. "You should allow yourself more time, young man."

"I'm after that bear in one of the middle carriages," said Peter. "He ran away from my cousin Betty, who loves him very much."

"Well, I hope you catch him," said the rabbit, opening a newspaper, and beginning to read. "You caught the train, so you seem quite good at catching, don't you?"

Peter wanted to ask him a lot of questions, but he didn't like to say any more, because the rabbit was reading so very solemnly. He looked round the truck. There were only two other passengers there, and one was a most unpleasant-looking rat. Peter felt that that he couldn't possibly ask him anything. The other passenger was a person rather like a wizard. He was fast asleep, and snored so loudly that he almost drowned the noise that the train was making.

For some time the train ran through long dark tunnels, and then came suddenly out into the open air. It went up a very steep hill, and ran down the other side so quickly that Peter had to clutch tightly to the sides of the truck, for he was almost tipped out. The wizard, who was still fast asleep, did not hold tight, and he *was* flung out.

"Ooh!" said Peter, in fright, "he's gone!"

"He's used to it," said the rabbit, glancing up from his paper. "He's always trying to get to a station a good bit ahead, but he never gets farther than here, because he falls asleep in that tunnel and gets pitched out on Sugar-Loaf Hill."

"But doesn't he hurt himself?" asked Peter, in surprise.

66

"You can't have known many wizards if you think they ever get hurt," said the rabbit, scornfully. He took off his glasses and put them carefully in a case.

"I get off at the next station," he said. "The one after that is Toyland, where your friend the bear will probably get out. Good-bye."

The train ran into a tiny station, and stopped just long enough for the rabbit and one or two other passengers to alight. Peter leaned over the side of his truck to see that the teddy didn't get out too. He saw the bear looking at him from one of the trucks in the middle, and he waved to him.

"Don't be afraid of me!" he cried. "Let me take you back to Betty."

The bear drew back his head, and the engine gave its funny little whistle. Off it went, and Peter watched the country they passed by. It was very pretty, for there was sunshine everywhere, and every meadow and hillside was full of bright flowers. All the trees bore gay flowers too, and Peter thought he had never seen anything quite so pretty.

Suddenly the countryside changed. The trees became stiff and wooden, and the farms were very prim and proper. The cows in the field walked about in jerks, and so did the farmer's men.

"Why, the trees look just like those on my toy farm at home!" said Peter, in surprise.

"What do you expect?" said the rat, in a sharp voice. "This is Toyland."

Peter said no more. He didn't like the look of

the rat at all. He had such sharp teeth and looked so hungry. Peter leaned out of the truck to see if Toyland Station was anywhere near. Away in the distance he saw it, and he made up his mind to keep a good look out to see if the teddy bear really *did* get out.

The train ran into the station. Peter kept a close watch to see who got out. He saw a mole carrying a bag, a gnome with a long beard, a sharp-eyed weasel, and a very prickly hedgehog. But no bear at all.

"That's funny," said Peter. "I suppose he must be getting out farther on."

The train began to start off again. Peter put his head in, and then looked at the rat, who was laughing loudly.

"Ho, ho!" he laughed. "The bear was too clever for you! He got out on the other side of the train, and ran across the line so that you shouldn't see him! See, there he goes!"

Peter looked to where the rat was pointing. Sure enough, there was the bear, running as fast as he could into a wood on the other side of the line.

"Why didn't you tell me before?" asked Peter, crossly. "Now I've lost him!"

But the train was not going very fast, and Peter suddenly thought he could jump out without hurting himself. So he opened the carriage door, and sprang off. He nearly rolled over, but just managed to save himself in time.

Then he ran after the bear. Into the wood he went, and hearing a panting noise some distance in front of him, he went that way. Soon he came to a doll's house set in the midst of the wood. There was no sign of the bear, so Peter thought that he must have gone into the house. He knocked at the door.

A very pretty little doll opened it, and stared in surprise at Peter.

"Is there a teddy bear living here?" asked Peter, politely.

"No," said the doll. "Oh, listen! What's that?"

Peter listened. He heard a curious noise like the sound of something being wound up.

"That's our clockwork motor car!" cried the doll. "Someone's stealing it!"

Peter ran round to where a tiny garage stood—just in time to see the teddy bear whizz out in a toy motor car!

"Oh, *bother*!" he cried. "I've just missed him again! I'm chasing that bear and can't seem to catch him at all!"

"Catch the bus that comes by in a few minutes!" cried the doll in excitement. "Our car can't go very fast."

"All right," said Peter. "Is that it?"

He pointed to where a bright red bus was coming along in the distance.

"Yes," said the doll. "The bear is sure to go the same way as the bus, because there is only one road through the wood, and this is it. Quick! Get on to the bus!"

Peter hopped on, waved good-bye to the doll, and sat down. No one came to ask him to pay his fare, and he was the only passenger. After some time he saw the motor car in front, with the bear driving it.

"I shall soon catch him!" thought Peter. But just as the bus came up to the motor, the bear turned into a side road and drove along it swiftly.

Peter pulled the cord to stop the bus—but it wouldn't stop! So he leapt off, sat down hard in the road, and tried to get his breath back. Then up he jumped and tore off into the side road after the bear.

He followed the marks of the wheels for a good way, and at last came to a tiny cottage. In front of it was the toy motor car, but there was no one in it.

"Well, he must have gone into that cottage," said Peter. "I'll creep up and see. I shan't knock at the door in case it warns him, and he runs off again."

So he crept up to a window and peeped in. Inside he saw a very queer sight.

There were two big bears there, and the little one he had been chasing. In a cradle lay a much smaller one. His bear was crying bitterly, and was being cuddled by one of the big bears.

"I'm so homesick," said the little bear. "Do let me stay at home, Mother."

"You know you can't," said the big bear. "This is very naughty of you, Teddy."

Peter jumped in at the window. The little bear gave a squeal and buried his face in his mother's arms.

70

"Excuse me," said Peter, politely. "But may I have that bear? He belongs to Betty, my cousin, and she would be dreadfully upset if she thought he was lost. She loves him very much."

"Oh, you naughty bear!" said his mother. "How dare you run away when someone loves you? Whatever made you do such a foolish thing?"

"I don't think he likes anyone except Betty to cuddle him," said Peter. "I picked him up, and he ran away from me. I wasn't going to hurt him, I only wanted to love him, you know. He is so cuddly."

"I am very much ashamed of him," said the father bear, in a deep voice. "I am afraid we have spoilt him. You know the story of the 'Three Bears' I expect? Well, I am the Father Bear, this is the Mother Bear, and your cousin's teddy is the Little Bear. We made a great fuss of him. He had his own little chair, his own little dish for porridge, and his own soft little bed. But he was naughty and grew up very spoilt."

"So when we had another baby bear, we decided he must be sent away," said the mother bear. "We gave him to Santa Claus to take to your cousin Betty, for we knew she was kind and would love him. But he is silly and very shy. We would be glad if you would take him back to Betty safely. Tell her to put butter on his feet every night for a week, and then he won't run away any more."

"I will," said Peter, feeling very much astonished to hear such a queer story. "Come along, teddy bear, you must be good and come back with me. Betty loves you, and wants you back."

The little bear hugged his mother hard, and then wiped his tears away.

"I'll be good now," he said. He came over to Peter and put his paw into the little boy's hand.

"How can we get back to the garden as quickly as possible?" asked Peter.

"I'll get the Spotted Woodpecker to take you," said the father bear. "He nests in the wood at the end of Betty's garden, and is a very old friend of ours. He used to bring us news of Little Bear every day."

He went outside and whistled three times. Down flew a beautiful spotted woodpecker, with a splash of red on his head.

"But we're much too big to get on to his back!" cried Peter.

"Try it and see!" said the father bear.

So Peter tried—and dear me, as soon as he touched the soft feathers of the woodpecker, he became very small, and so did the teddy bear. They sat on the bird's back, and held tightly. Up he went into the air, and they waved good-bye to the two bears below.

In a very short time they were over Betty's garden. Down they went to the grass. Peter jumped off, and pulled the bear with him. At once they both shot up to their right size, and the woodpecker seemed very small indeed.

"Isn't that wonderful!" said Peter, feeling rather

giddy. "Betty! Betty! Where are you? I've got such an adventure to tell you!"

Betty came running up.

"Wherever have you been?" she cried. "I've been looking everywhere for you! Oh, and there's my darling teddy bear! I was so afraid he might have run away again!"

"That's just what he did do, and I went after him!" said Peter. He told Betty all that had happened, and she sat nursing the bear in the greatest astonishment.

"Oh, the naughty little bear!" she said. "However shall I teach him that he mustn't run away any more?"

"Put butter on the soles of his feet every night for a week," said Peter. "That's what his mother advised you to do."

So for seven nights Betty buttered her teddy bear's feet—and he has never once run away again, and she really doesn't think he will now.

If *your* teddy ever does the same, just remember to put butter on his feet. You may be sure that will quite cure him.

In Nursery-Rhyme Land

Betty and John had a lovely wall-paper in their nursery. It showed all the nursery-rhyme folk going about their work. There were Jack and Jill going up the hill, Tommy Tucker singing for his supper, Little Bo-peep looking for her sheep, and many, many others.

Betty and John were never tired of looking at their wall-paper. There were trees and hills on it, and little round ponds with ducks. There were funny houses, and there was a Noah's Ark floating on a river, with Mr. and Mrs. Noah looking out of the window. A great many of the animals were peeping out of the top, and they all looked very happy. It really was a *lovely* wall-paper.

"Don't you wish we could visit the land on our

wall-paper?" asked Betty one day. "It does look so exciting, and we should be able to meet so many nursery-rhyme folk!"

John wished they could, too, but he felt certain that they never would. Things like that never seemed to happen.

But one evening, as they were sitting over the fire reading a book, John happened to look up at the wall-paper—and he saw a very strange thing.

All the people on it were moving! Jack and Jill were really walking up the hill, the Noah's Ark was really floating along the river, and Little Jack Horner was really eating his pie!

"I must be dreaming!" said John, in the greatest surprise. "I say, Betty! Look at the wall-paper! Does it seem different to you?"

Betty looked, and then she jumped to her feet in astonishment.

"Why, all the people are alive!" she cried. "Oh, John! Let's call Mummy!"

"No, don't let's," said John. "The wall-paper would go quite ordinary again as soon as she came in. I know it would. Let's go nearer and look at it. Oh, Betty! Isn't it queer!"

The two children ran close to the paper, and looked at it. There was no doubt that everyone on it was moving.

"It doesn't look like a paper now," said Betty. "It looks like real land, only very far away. Oh, John, John! It's suddenly getting bigger!"

John caught hold of Betty's hand, and held it

75

tight. Yes, everything in the paper was getting very large. Whatever was going to happen?

The two children stood quite still and stared hard. In front of them was a little house, and this seemed to be getting nearly as big as a real house. Soon it was so big that the children couldn't see anything else at all. It hid everything.

"John! It's not a paper house, it's *real*!" said Betty. "Look, the chimney's smoking! Something very strange has happened. Oh, dear, it's rather frightening—but isn't it *exciting*!"

"Where's the nursery?" said John, looking behind him. "Why, Betty, it's gone! We're standing in the garden of the little house! It must be magic, really it must!"

Sure enough the nursery was gone. The children were standing on a tiny path in front of the little house they had so often seen on their wall-paper. They had wondered who lived there, for the door was shut, and there was no one looking out of the window.

"Well, we've often wanted an adventure, and now we've got one!" said John. "Let's enjoy it, Betty!"

The sun was shining all around them, which was very queer, because it had been evening time in the nursery. It seemed about midday, and was very hot.

"We can't stand on this garden path all day," said John. "What shall we do, Betty?"

Just as he said that the door of the cottage opened,

and out came a little girl with a bowl of curds and whey in her hands.

"It's Little Miss Muffet!" said John, in excitement. "Now we know who lives in this cottage, Betty."

"Good morning," said Little Miss Muffet. "What are you doing on my garden path? Did you want to see me?"

"No," said John. "We just found ourselves here. Please excuse us. We are very glad to see you."

"That's nice of you," said Miss Muffet. "Come with me. I'll show you a dear little tuffet of grass that I always sit on every day to eat my curds and whey."

She ran down the path and out of the gate. The two children followed her. She took them to a little wood, and there, under the trees, was a small grassy seat, just high enough for a little girl to sit on. Miss Muffet sat down, and smiled at Betty and John.

"Would you like to sit on it just once?" she asked Betty. Betty said yes, she would love to. So down she sat, thinking what a dear little tuffet it was.

But suddenly John began to shout and scream.

"Get up, Betty! Quick, get up! Here's the spider! Oh quick! It's the biggest I've ever seen!"

Betty jumped up in a dreadful hurry. Sure enough, letting itself down from a tree just over Betty's head, was a spider nearly as big as Betty herself! Miss Muffet screamed and ran away, leaving her curds and whey beside the tuffet. Betty ran too, and John caught hold of her hand and ran with her.

When they had run a long way, they turned and looked back. The spider was sitting on the tuffet, eating Miss Muffet's curds and whey!

"Just fancy that!" cried John. "He does that every day, I expect. If I were Miss Muffet I wouldn't go and sit on that tuffet any more, would you, Betty?"

"No," said Betty, with a shiver, for she didn't very much like spiders. "Miss Muffet's gone, John. I expect she went back to her little house. Come on, let's go and find someone else."

They went on down a little winding lane. Soon they came to a small boy sitting in a corner of a field, eating a big pie. He had very bad manners, for instead of using a spoon, he put in his thumb and finger, and pulled the plums out with them.

"It's Little Jack Horner!" whispered Betty.

"What a good boy am I!" said Jack Horner, popping a great big plum into his mouth. "Hullo, you two! Where are you going?"

"We don't know," said John. "We're just wandering about."

"Oh, well, mind you don't get caught by the Old Woman Who Lives in a Shoe," said Jack Horner, taking out another plum, and popping it into his mouth. "She's lost some of her children, and she's out looking for them. If she catches you, you'll have a very bad time. She feeds them on butter without any bread, and whips them all soundly and sends them to bed."

"Good gracious!" said John, in alarm. "Do you really think she would try and catch us, Jack?"

"Rather!" said Jack. "She tried to get me yesterday, but I got the Cow with the Crumpled Horn to frighten her off. The old cow is a great friend of mine, you know. She lives in this field. Look, there she is."

John and Betty looked. They saw a fat brown cow grazing nearby. One of her horns was all crumpled. She looked at them with her great eyes, and then went on grazing.

"Hie! Look out! There's the Old Woman!" suddenly cried Jack Horner. John and Betty looked round quickly. They saw an old woman coming up the lane, carrying in her hand the birch with which she whipped her children.

John caught hold of Betty's hand, and ran for his life. The old woman saw them, and at once began to run after them.

"Come here, you naughty children!" she cried. "I've been looking for you everywhere. Come back to the Shoe at once."

Betty and John tore down the lane. They turned the corner, and came to a little cottage. The front door was open, so without thinking, they ran into it, shut the door, and then peeped out of the window. The Old Woman soon came by. She stopped at the gate and looked all about. John and Betty trembled—but she didn't come in.

Instead she stood at the gate as if she was waiting for someone.

Soon that someone came. It was a little girl carrying a doll, and she came dancing to the gate and opened it. Then the Old Woman stretched out her hand and took hold of her shoulder.

"You're one of my lost children!" she said, in a very cross voice.

"Indeed I'm not!" said the little girl, tossing her head. "I'm Mary, Mary, Quite Contrary, and this is my house and garden. Take your hand off me, Old Woman, and go away!"

"You rude little girl!" said the Old Woman. "It will do you good to come and live in my Shoe for a while. You shall come with me and learn manners!"

Mary began to cry, but it was no good. Off she had to go with the Old Woman. Betty and John looked on in dismay, very glad to think they had not been caught too.

"This must be Mary Quite Contrary's garden," said John. "Look, there are the silver bells hung on sticks, and all the beds are edged with cockle shells. But what are those dolls sitting out there?"

"Why, those are the pretty maids all in a row!" said Betty. "Don't you remember the nursery rhyme, John?"

"Oh, yes," said John. "Well, come on, Betty. We'd better leave here, and go on again. What an adventure this is!"

"I do hope we don't meet that horrid Old

Woman again!" said Betty. "I'd like to see the Noah's Ark, wouldn't you, John?"

"Yes," said John. "Let's ask the way to the river."

So when they met Little Bo-peep looking for her sheep, they asked her the way, and she told them.

"You don't happen to have seen my sheep, do you?" she asked. "I keep losing them, the naughty things."

"No, we haven't seen any sheep at all," said John. "Only a cow with a crumpled horn."

On they went again, and soon came to the river. And there, floating on the water, was the Noah's Ark. Mr. and Mrs. Noah were looking out of the window, and all the animals were peeping out of the top, just as they had done in the wall-paper. But now they were very big, and the Ark was like a great house.

"Good morning!" cried Mr. and Mrs. Noah. "Do come in and see us! We'll send the hippo over to you, and you can climb on his back. Then he will carry you across."

All the animals began to bellow and roar, howl and bark, and Betty and John felt a bit frightened.

"I don't think we will, thank you," said John. "The animals don't seem to want us."

"Bless you, that's only their way of saying 'Do come!' " said Mrs. Noah. "*They* won't hurt you."

But the lion looked rather fierce, and John and Betty really thought that the Ark was much too crowded for them to visit it. So they said no thank you again quite firmly, and then ran down the river-path as fast as they could.

All the animals looked after them, and for a long time they made such a noise that John and Betty couldn't hear anything else. Soon they came to a little hill, and ran up the winding path to the top. Then who should they see coming down but Jack and Jill carrying a full pail of water between them.

Just as Jack and Jill came up to them, Jill tripped on a stone and over she went, dragging Jack with her. The pail spilt all its water, and Jack began to howl.

"Oh dear, I *thought* you'd fall over!" said Betty. "You always do in our picture books. Never mind, get up and I'll bind your forehead with a nice clean handkerchief."

She tied her handkerchief right round Jack's head and he soon stopped crying. Jill thanked Betty very much, and asked her where she was going. But before Betty could answer, Jack gave a yell.

"Look! There's the Old Woman who lives in a Shoe! Look out, or she'll catch us!"

At once Jack and Jill tore down the hill, and soon disappeared. John looked round and saw the Old Woman very near to them. Betty took hold of John's hand, and very quickly the two children ran away from her again.

But alas for them! The path they took led to the river! It ended there, and there was no further way except by going into the water. Betty and

John didn't know what to do. They saw the Noah's Ark away in the distance, but it was too far off to be of any help.

The Old Woman came panting after them. She took hold of their hands and held them tight.

"Why do you run away, you naughty children?" she scolded. "I have been looking for you all morning."

"We aren't your children," said John. "You must let us go."

"*Must* indeed!" said the Old Woman. "You are like Mary Quite Contrary. You need to learn manners. I've whipped her and put her to bed, the naughty little girl. Come along with me, and have your broth without any bread."

Betty began to cry, and John to struggle, but it was no use. The old Woman was just as strong as their Daddy was and they couldn't get away. They had to go with her.

They saw Little Tommy Tucker singing for his supper, and Tom Tom the Piper's Son, and Little Red Riding Hood on the way, but although John called to them to come and rescue them, they didn't do anything of the sort. They just ran away as fast as their legs could carry them.

Betty was still crying.

"Oh, John!" she said, "Nursery-Rhyme Land would be lovely without the Old Woman Who Lived in a Shoe. I do wish we were back in our own nursery, don't you?"

"Yes, I do," said John. "But it's no use wishing."

But it *was* some use! No sooner had the two

children wished their wish than something funny happened. The houses and fields began to get smaller and smaller, the paths narrower, and the people very tiny. Only the Old Woman seemed just as big as ever. She held them by the arm, and they couldn't get away.

Smaller and smaller grew the Land of Nursery Rhyme—or was it that Betty and John grew larger and larger? They didn't know. Then suddenly it wasn't a Land any more—but just a big flat stretch of wall-paper, with houses and fields, ponds, river and people painted on it. They were in their nursery!

But the Old Woman still held their arms tightly. Had she come to their nursery with them? John and Betty turned round to tell her that if she didn't let them go they would call for their mother.

And oh dear me, what a surprise! It wasn't the Old Woman after all, but Mummy herself, smiling at them.

"Well, you've been standing looking at your wall-paper so long that I really thought you'd gone to sleep!" she said. "Come along, my dears, it's bath-time, and the water's lovely and hot."

"Oh Mummy, we thought you were the Old Woman Who Lived in a Shoe!" said John. "I'm *so* glad you're not!"

"Well, where did she go to?" asked Betty, staring at Mummy in surprise. "She was here a minute ago."

"Oh, so you *have* been asleep, then, and dreaming too!" laughed Mummy.

"No we haven't, Mummy," said Betty. "We've been to the Nursery-Rhyme Country in the wallpaper, and we had the most exciting adventures!"

But Mummy wouldn't believe her, so Betty says that next time she goes, she will ask Mary Quite Contrary for a silver bell and a cockle shell from her garden—and then Mummy will know for certain it's all as true as true can be!

The Castle without a Door

ONCE upon a time a wizard came to live just outside Brownie Town. He was called Kookle, and no one knew much about him.

"He's building himself a castle on the hill," they said to one another. "He just sits on a stone and says queer words, and the castle grows out of the ground. It is wonderful to watch."

"But it's a very queer castle," said Tinker, a fat, jolly brownie. "Do you know that it hasn't any doors at all? How are people going to get in and out, that's what I'd like to know. The windows are far too high up to climb into."

"That's very funny," said the brownies, and they shook their heads. "Perhaps Kookle is up to mischief of some sort."

It wasn't long before Kookle was very much

disliked. He never spoke to the brownies at all, not even when they wished him good day. He turned one of them into a pillar-box one day because the little brownie had accidentally run into him round a corner, and it took Brownie Town a whole week before they could find the right magic to turn the pillar-box back into a brownie.

"He is a horrid wizard," said the little folk. "If only we could get rid of him! But what can you do with someone who lives in a castle without any doors? You can't even get in and beg him not to hurt us!"

"He'll do worse mischief yet, you mark my words!" said Tinker.

Now two weeks after that, little Princess Peronel came to stay with her old nurse, Mother Browneyes, in the little cottage at the west end of Brownie Town. She loved her old nurse, and the two of them went walking in Wishing Wood every day. And then suddenly a dreadful thing happened.

Mother Browneyes came running back from Wishing Wood in a terrible state, crying and groaning in distress.

"What's the matter, what's the matter?" cried the brownies.

"Oh, oh!" wept Mother Browneyes. "I was in the wood this morning, when who should come up but Kookle the Wizard. And no sooner did he set eyes on pretty little Peronel than he said: 'Ha! I will have you marry me!' And oh, whatever shall we do? He caught her up then and there and carried her off to his castle!"

"Goodness gracious! What a terrible thing!" cried all the brownies in horror. "Our little Princess with that horrid old wizard! Whatever can we do?"

Well, they decided to go at once to the castle and demand Peronel back. So they trooped off, scores of them, all feeling very angry but a good deal frightened too, in case Kookle should turn them into beetles or frogs.

They arrived at the castle, and then of course they remembered it had no doors. They couldn't knock because there was no knocker, and they couldn't ring because there was no bell. They just stood there round the castle and wondered what in the world they could do.

"Hie! Hie!" suddenly shouted Tinker, the fat little brownie. "Kookle! Kookle! If you're anywhere in the castle, just listen to what we say. Give us back Peronel at once!"

Suddenly the wizard appeared at a window and looked down at the brownies. He laughed loudly.

"Ho!" he cried. "If you want Peronel, come in and get her. Ho ho ho!"

"We can't," yelled Tinker in a rage. "There are no doors!"

"Then go away!" said the wizard. "If you're not all gone by the time I count ten, I'll turn you into muffin-bells! Ha ha! Now—one, two, three . . ."

But by the time Kookle came to ten, there wasn't a single brownie to be seen. They had all fled down the hill to the town.

"We *must* do something," said they. "We can't

let Peronel be captured like this. What shall we do? Shall we send for the King's army?"

"Pooh, what's the good of that?" asked Tinker. "Do you want them all turned into mice or something? No, until we know where the door of the castle is, there's not a single thing we can do."

"But there *is* no door," said another brownie.

"There must be one that we can't see," said Tinker. "The wizard comes in and out, doesn't he? Well, there simply *must* be a door, but by some kind of magic he has hidden it from our eyes. What we must do is to find out where it is, and then, even if we can't see it, we shall know where to find it and can turn the handle by feeling about for it."

"Well, couldn't we go to the castle to-night and feel all round the walls for the door?" said the other brownies.

"Yes," said Tinker. So that night six brownies went creeping up to the castle and began to feel round the wall. But alas for them! The wizard heard them, and turned them all into kittens, so that Brownie Town was in despair to see six little kittens come running back that night, instead of six brownies.

Tinker sat down in his cottage and thought very hard. He did so want to rescue Peronel, for he thought she was the prettiest little Princess in all Fairyland. But try as he would he could think of no plan.

Next morning when Brownie Town awoke and drew its curtains back, it saw that snow had fallen in the night, and all the countryside was white.

"Hurrah!" cried the youngsters. "Now we can build snowmen and play with snowballs."

Then Tinker suddenly had a wonderful idea, and he ran out of his cottage to tell the others.

"Come round and listen," he said. "I have a plan."

Everyone came close, and listened to Tinker.

"We will build a big snowman in the field just outside the castle," he said. "If the wizard sees us doing that he will take no notice. But listen! In the night, before the moon is out, I will dress myself in a white cloak, and put on the snowman's hat. You shall quickly knock down the snowman and I will take his place! Then I will stand there all night and watch to see where the door is when the wizard comes out for his nightly walk!"

"Oh, Tinker, how clever you are!" cried all the others. "That is a wonderful plan! Kookle will never guess that you are not a real snowman!"

"Six of you go and make the snowman now," said Tinker. "Make him about my size. Laugh and talk all the time, as if you were really playing and had forgotten all about Peronel."

So six of the brownies went off to the hill on which Kookle's castle stood. They laughed and talked, and looked as if they hadn't a care in the world. The wizard peeped out of one of his windows, but when he saw them playing with the snow and building a snowman, he took no further notice.

Before night came the brownies had built a nice fat snowman just about Tinker's size. They put a row of stones down his front for buttons, and tied a muffler round his neck. They put a hat with a feather in it on his head, and stuck a pipe in his mouth. Then he was finished.

Off they went down the hill to Brownie Town. Tinker had been very busy all day long making himself a long white cloak. Mother Browneyes had helped him, and together they had sewn six big black buttons down the front. When night came, the cloak was ready.

The six brownies ran into the cottage.

"We've finished the snowman!" they cried. "It's just your size, Tinker. Hurry up before the moon shines out. We'll go back with you and help you."

So in the darkness before the moon rose the seven brownies went silently back up the hill. When they came to their snowman they quickly knocked it down, and Tinker stood in its place with his long white cloak round him.

The brownies wound the snowman's muffler round his neck and put the snowman's feathered hat on his head. They stuck the pipe in his mouth and he was ready!

"Ooh!" said the brownies. "You *do* look like a snowman, Tinker! Nobody could possibly tell that you weren't one! Well, good-bye and good luck to you! The moon is just coming up and we must go."

They ran down the snowy hill, and Tinker was left alone. He felt rather lonely and frightened. Suppose the wizard guessed he wasn't a real snowman? Ooh, that would be dreadful!

The moon came up and soon Tinker could see

every brick of the castle quite clearly. There he stood on the hillside, hat on head, and pipe in mouth, standing as still as could be, his white cloak reaching down to his heels. He waited for an hour He waited for two hours. He waited for three, and four and five. He waited until midnight, and by that time he was so cold that he was shivering.

"Oh my, I do hope the wizard won't see me shivering," thought Tinker in a fright. "But I can't help it. I can't stop shaking with the cold!"

Now just at that moment the clock down in Brownie Town struck twelve. Tinker heard it— and at the same time he heard a voice inside the castle chanting a long string of magic words. And then, before his eyes, he saw the door of the castle appearing! It was outlined in green flame, and he saw it quite clearly. There was a knocker and a handle, and a very big letter-box.

As Tinker watched with his eyes wide open in surprise, he saw the door swing open. The wizard appeared in the opening, and stood there for one moment before stepping outside. Tinker hurriedly counted the number of bricks from the side of the castle to the door, for he knew that at any moment the door might disappear again. His heart was thumping so loudly he was afraid the wizard would hear it.

Kookle stepped outside, and at the same moment the door faded away and disappeared. The place where it had been looked just like the wall again. Then suddenly Kookle looked towards Tinker!

"Ha, a snowman!" said the wizard. "Stupid

little brownies! How they do waste their time! I've a good mind to knock it all down!"

Tinker nearly died of fright. The wizard came right up to him and snatched the pipe out of his mouth. What Kookle meant to do next Tinker didn't know—but just at that very moment a witch came sailing through the air on her broom stick and called loudly to the wizard.

"Hey, Kookle! It's time to join the big meeting. Come along!"

In a trice the wizard left Tinker by himself, leapt on to the broom with the witch, and sailed off into the moonlit sky. Tinker sighed with relief, and began to tremble, for he had been very much frightened. As soon as the wizard was quite out of sight he threw off his cloak, and ran to the castle. He counted fifty-three bricks from the side of the castle, and then began to feel about for the door.

Almost at once he felt the handle and the knocker. He turned the handle and the door swung open. He stepped into the castle and shut the door.

"Peronel! Peronel!" he cried. "Where are you?"

"Here! Here!" cried a tiny voice, far away. "Oh who are you? Have you come to save me? I am right at the top of the castle!"

Tinker ran to the winding staircase, and raced up it, two steps at a time. He had to stop to get his breath after he had gone up some way, for there were many hundreds of stairs. Up he went, and up and up, hoping with all his heart that Kookle would not return until he had got the Princess away in safety.

At the top of the castle was a small tower. In this Peronel was imprisoned. Her door was locked and bolted on the outside, and Tinker quickly drew the big bolts back, and turned the key, which the wizard had left in the lock.

In the tower room was the little Princess, very pale and thin, for the wizard had given her only bread and water because she would not consent to marry him. She ran to Tinker and flung her arms round his neck.

"Oh, you dear, brave brownie!" she cried. "Thank you so much for saving me!"

"You're not saved yet!" said Tinker. "Quick, we must get out of the castle before the wizard comes back."

Down the hundreds of stairs they ran, and then went to the big door, which was quite easily seen from the inside of the castle. And then, oh dear, how dreadful! Tinker couldn't open the door! No matter how he twisted the handle and pulled, that door wouldn't open! The little brownie was in despair.

For two hours he tried to get out, but at last he gave it up. The door was closed by magic and only the right magic words could open it from the inside.

"What *are* we to do?" said the Princess, almost in tears. "Kookle will soon be back, and then we shall be in a worse fix than before. He will be terribly angry."

"I know what we'll do!" said Tinker at last. "It

isn't a very good plan I've thought of, but it might work. I expect the wizard will see that the snowman is gone and guess that I am here. He will come rushing into the castle in a fearful rage, and race up to the tower. Well, look—I've got some string here. I'll tie it from this stool to that chair over there, and when the wizard comes in it will trip him up and perhaps we shall just have time to run out of the castle."

"Yes, that's a good plan," said Peronel. "And, Tinker, don't let's try to run all the way down the hill to Brownie Town, because the wizard is sure to catch us. Just outside you will see a rabbit hole. Well, Sandy, a very nice bunny lives there, and I know he would let us shelter in his burrow till the danger is past."

"That's splendid," said Tinker. He quickly tied the string across the hall just beyond the doorway. Then, hearing a cock crow in Brownie Town, and knowing that the wizard would soon be returning, he and Peronel crouched down in a dark corner near the door.

Suddenly they heard the sound of an angry voice outside. It was the wizard, who had discovered the snowman's cloak on the ground, and had seen that the snowman was gone.

"What's this! What's this!" he cried in a fury. "This is a trick! That snowman was a brownie, and he saw me come from the castle! Well, he can't get out, and I'll catch him, yes, I will!"

In another moment the door flew open, and the wizard rushed in. He caught his foot against the string and down he fell with a crash! The door began to close, but Peronel and Tinker slipped through in a flash, and then tore down the hill. The Princess led the brownie to a rabbit hole, and the two crept down it. The bunny came to meet them, and they explained to him in a whisper that they were in danger and needed shelter.

"Come this way," said Sandy, and he led them to a little round room, where there was a tiny fire and a jugful of cocoa warming by it.

"Help yourselves to the cocoa," said Sandy. "And there are biscuits in that tin. I'm just going back to the hillside to see what is happening. Don't be afraid. You are quite safe here."

So Tinker poured out a steaming hot cup of cocoa for Peronel, and gave her some sugar-biscuits. Then he helped himself, for he was hungry and cold. They sat there, warm and happy, till Sandy the Rabbit came back.

"Ha!" said Sandy in glee. "That old wizard is in a dreadful temper. He bumped his head when he fell down, and hurt his knee. He tore down the hillside after you, but of course he didn't know you had come here. He couldn't find you, so he's gone back to his castle to bathe his head. I shouldn't be surprised to find that he leaves Brownie Town quite soon."

All that night the brownie and Peronel stayed with the kind rabbit. Next morning they followed Sandy down many long winding passages underground that led to the bottom of the hill. There they came out into the sunshine and said good-bye

He caught his foot against the string, and down he fell with a crash!

to the rabbit. Off they went to Brownie Town, the Princess skipping for joy to be free again.

What a welcome they got! How all the brownies cheered! And how pleased old Mother Browneyes was to see the Princess again!

Just as they were all as happy as could be, listening to Tinker's adventures, there came a big BANG! Everyone rushed out to see what was happening—and a very queer sight they saw!

Kookle the Wizard had made up his mind to leave Brownie Town, and had worked a spell on his castle. With a big BANG it had risen into the air and was now sailing away to the east, flapping two huge wings that had grown out of the walls.

"Ooh!" said all the brownies in surprise and joy. "That's the end of the old wizard! He'll never come again! Let's give a party this afternoon to show we're happy!"

So they did, and the Princess sat next to Tinker, who was happier than he had ever been in his life before. And when Peronel presented him with a lovely gold watch for saving her, you should have heard all the brownies cheer! It was the jolliest afternoon you can imagine—and I *do* wish I'd been there, don't you?

The Tale of Higgle and Hum

ONCE upon a time the King of Fairyland went to his magic cupboard and found that a thief had been there in the night.

"My goodness!" cried the King, in a loud voice. "Robbers! Now what have they taken?"

He called the Queen and together they went through all the things in the magic cupboard, and they found that three had been stolen.

"There's my magic lamp gone!" said the King in dismay. "The one that lights up the whole of the wood when the moon doesn't shine for our dances."

"And where are my magic scissors?" said the Queen, with a groan. "The pair that will cut through anything—iron, steel or stone!"

"And my fine walking stick," said the King, sadly. "I'm sorry that has been stolen, because I had only to say, 'Up, stick, and at him!' and it would jump up and beat any rogue I met."

"How shall we get our things back?" wondered the Queen. "And who has taken them?"

They soon found out who the thief was. It was a goblin called Groo, a cunning fellow who had long wanted these three things for himself.

"He is so clever that I am afraid we shall never have our magic things again," said the Queen, with a sigh. "If we sent our soldiers against him, he would simply turn them all into an army of ants, and that would be dreadful."

"Well, we'll send out a proclamation saying that if anyone can get back our magic things for us we will give him a sack of gold, a beautiful palace and a free invitation to all our dances and parties," said the King.

So this was done, and soon all the elves, pixies, fairies, gnomes and brownies were talking excitely of how the three things belonging to the King might be taken from Groo the Goblin.

First an elf tried, and, oh dear me, he was turned into a frog, and it took the King a very long time to find the right spell that would change him back into his own shape again. Then two gnomes tried and they were turned into earwigs. They went to the King in a fright, and he had to pay a wise man twenty pieces of gold to change them back again.

After that no one tried, for everyone was afraid.

Then one day there came wandering into Fairyland two imps called Higgle and Hum. As soon as they heard of the King's message they looked at one another in delight.

"*We'll* get the things back!" they cried.

"Easier said than done!" said a listening brownie. "You don't know how clever Groo the Goblin is!"

Higgle and Hum said no more, but went off to a sunny hedge-side to talk about how they should get into Groo's house.

"We've been poor and ragged all our lives," said Higgle, "and we've never had a chance of being rich, or having nice shoes and clothes. Why, we haven't ever been to a party or a dance, because we were so raggedy! How fine it would be to have a sack of gold and live in a palace on a hill! And oh, think of going to every single party that the King and Queen give! What a fine time we should have!"

"How shall we get the magic things, though?" asked Hum. "Hadn't we better make a plan?"

They thought and thought, and at last decided that it wasn't a bit of good making a plan—they had just better see what they could do, and make plans as they went along.

That night they crept into the garden of Groo's house, and peered in through the kitchen window.

"Look!" whispered Higgle. "There's the magic lamp on the dresser!"

"And there's the magic scissors in that work-basket!" said Hum. "Where's the magic stick?"

"Standing in the corner yonder," whispered Higgle. "Oh! Oh! Oh!"

It was no wonder he cried out "Oh!" for someone had suddenly caught hold of him! It was Groo the Goblin, and very soon he had Higgle in one hand and Hum in the other, both imps trembling with fright.

"Ho!" he said in a harsh voice. "What are you doing peeping and prying into my kitchen, I should like to know? Don't you know that I can turn people into earwigs and frogs, if I want to?"

"Please, please don't do that!" said Higgle, in a fright. "We were thinking what a nice warm kitchen you had, and wondering if you wanted any servants."

"Well, my wife could do with two," said Groo. "I'll show you to her and see if she wants you. If she doesn't I'll have you cooked for my dinner."

He took the shivering imps into his kitchen and showed them to his wife, who looked at them through her big glasses.

"Yes, they'll do nicely, dear," she said to Groo. "I'll have them for servants."

"Well, if you get tired of them, let me know and I'll have them cooked for dinner," said Groo. "And mind, wife, don't you let them get away! They'll run if they have a chance, I'm sure of that. You keep them safely in the kitchen."

"Very well, dear," said Mrs. Groo, and she turned to Higgle and Hum. "Just draw some hot water from the tap and start to scrub the kitchen floor," she said.

Groo the Goblin went out of the room and banged the door. Higgle and Hum ran to the tap and got a pail of water. It was not very hot, and Higgle looked at the fire.

"Please, Mam," he said to Mrs. Groo, "the water isn't hot enough to scrub the floor properly. The fire has gone down and the water is cooling. Shall I stoke it up?"

"Oh dear, oh dear, there's no wood in the wood-box," said the old dame in a flurry. "I meant to have asked Groo this morning to chop some for me, and I quite forgot. What a temper he will be in when I ask him now, for he does hate to go out to the woodshed in the dark."

"Well, Mam, let *me* go, said Higgle. "I'm your servant, aren't I?"

"Of course!" said Mrs. Groo. "Well, out you go and chop me some wood—but don't be long."

Higgle grinned at Hum and ran out. He didn't go to the woodshed, but hid outside the front gate. Soon Mrs. Groo became impatient and wondered whatever Higgle was doing.

"Drat the imp!" she said. "I suppose I must go and see if he's lost his way in the garden."

"Mam, let *me* go and find him!" said Hum, running over to her. "Don't you go out in the darkness! Lend me that lamp on the dresser, and I'll soon find him!"

"Well, take it, and don't be long," said Mrs. Groo. She lighted the lamp and Hum took it. He ran out into the garden, puffed out the lamp, and made for the front gate. He found Higgle there, and together the two clever imps raced down the lane as fast as their legs would carry them, rejoicing that their trick had succeeded.

The King was delighted to get his magic lamp, and he praised the two imps for being able to outwit the cunning old goblin.

"If only you can get the other things I shall be overjoyed!" said the Queen.

So the next night Higgle and Hum made their way quietly to Groo's house again, meaning to break in at the window when Groo had gone to bed, and take the scissors and magic stick. But the goblin was lying in wait for them, and pounced on the two scared imps just as they reached the front gate.

"Ha!" he said, "now I've got you again, and I can tell you, I won't let you go *this* time! I'll have you for my dinner to-morrow!"

He dragged the imps into the kitchen and shut them into the wood-box for the night. They could not get out, and they trembled there in fear, thinking that their end was very near this time. In the morning Mrs. Groo took them out and looked at them.

"You are very naughty not to have come back the night I sent you to chop the wood," she said. "Now I've got to cook you for my husband's dinner, instead of having you for servants!"

The imps watched her stoke up the fire and trembled all the more. Then Higgle spoke.

"I suppose, Mam, you've got plenty of killy-kolly leaves to cook with us?" he said. "If imps are cooked without killy-kolly leaves, they will poison whoever eats them."

"My goodness!" said Mrs. Groo in a fright. "No, I didn't know that! Well, I've plenty of killy-kollies in my garden. I'd better go and pick some."

"Let *me* pick them for you," said Higgle. "You've plenty to do in preparing the dinner, I'm sure."

"All right, you may go and pick them," said Mrs. Groo, giving him a plate. "But see that you keep in sight of the window, for if you run off again, Mr. Groo will be very angry."

Higgle took the plate, grinned at Hum and ran out into the garden to the killy-kolly bed. He began to pick some of the leaves, and he pretended that they were very hard indeed to pull from the stems. Mrs. Groo became impatient, and called out of the window to him.

"Hurry up, now, hurry up! I'm waiting for that dish of leaves. What a time you take picking them!"

"Please, Mam, they're very hard to pick," said Higgle, standing up in the killy-kolly bed. "Could you send Hum out with a pair of strong scissors? Then I could cut the leaves off easily, and bring them in to you at once."

Mrs. Groo went to her work-basket and took out the pair of magic scissors there. She gave them to Hum and bade him take them to Higgle, and then come back to help her peel some potatoes. Hum ran off, and as soon as Higgle saw him coming he ran to the front gate, and down the lane the two imps tore as fast as they could.

How glad they were to be free, and to have the magic scissors! They took them to the King and he was delighted.

"You're a very clever pair!" he said. "Now if only you can get me my magic stick, I shall be very happy."

The two imps didn't dare to go near Groo's house at once, for they knew he would be on the watch for them. But at last, after ten days had gone by, Higgle and Hum went once more to the goblin's house, and this time they crept in at the back way.

But, oh dear me, who should spy them but old Mrs. Groo, and she caught them and dragged them into her kitchen.

"So it's you again!" she said. "Well, you ran away last time with the magic scissors, and the time before with the magic lamp—but this time you *won't* get away! Mr. Groo will be pleased with me now for catching you!"

"Where *is* Groo?" asked Higgle, looking round.

"He's gone to see his friend Mr. Topple," said Mrs. Groo, "but don't you fret! He won't be long, I can tell you, and I shouldn't be surprised if he has you for his supper as soon as he comes home."

Higgle and Hum were frightened. They felt quite sure that they really would be eaten this time, and they tried in vain to think of some way of escape.

Mrs. Groo sat down to her sewing, and for

some time there was silence in the warm kitchen. Then the clock struck nine, and Mrs. Groo looked up in surprise.

"Dear dear!" she said, "how late Groo is! I do hope he hasn't got lost on this dark night."

"Shall I go and look for him?" asked Higgle.

"No, that you won't!" said Mrs. Groo, sharply.

"Well, Mam, just let me go to the front door and peep out," said Higgle. "You can see I don't escape then, can't you, but as I have very sharp eyes, I can see a long way and could tell you if your husband is coming."

"Very well," said Mrs. Groo, "but mind—if you so much as put a foot over the doorstep, I'll drag you in and put you into that saucepan, Higgle."

Higgle grinned at Hum and went to the door to open it. He stood on the doorstep and peered this way and that. Suddenly he gave a shout.

"Robbers! Thieves!" he cried. "Look, robbers, thieves! Where's a stick! Bring a stick to beat them with!"

Mrs. Groo began to tremble. She picked up the magic stick that stood in the corner and gave it to Hum, who ran to Higgle with it.

Sure enough, someone was coming up the front path, and Mrs. Groo felt certain it must be robbers. She began to scream.

"Up, stick, and at him!" shouted Higgle, and at once the stick leapt from his hand and flew at the person coming up the path. How it beat him and whipped him! And how he yelled and shouted.

"I'm no robber, I'm Groo the Goblin! Call the stick off, call it off! I'm Groo the Goblin, I tell you!"

But Higgle and Hum shouted too, so loudly that Mrs. Groo couldn't hear that it was her husband in the garden and not a robber. She hid herself in a corner, and didn't dream of calling the stick off.

Higgle and Hum ran to the back gate and half-way down the lane, grinning to think that the wicked goblin was having such a fine whipping.

Then Higgle put his hands to his mouth and shouted loudly:

"Stick, stick, come to me!"

The stick stopped beating Groo and flew to Higgle's hand. The two imps set off running as fast as they could, and the goblin was so sore with his beating that he could not run after them, but could only stumble into his kitchen and sit down on a chair.

How delighted the King and Queen were to see their magic stick safely back again!

"Surely you are the two cleverest imps in the kingdom!" said the King. "Well, you shall have your sack of gold, and your palace, and you may be sure you will receive a free invitation to every party and dance that the Queen gives. Thank you very much for all you have done."

Then in delight the two imps took the gold and went to the palace that the King gave them. They bought themselves splendid new suits, took two pretty little wives, and lived happily in their glittering palace for ever after. They still go to every party in Fairyland, and though they must have been to thousands now, they haven't got tired of them yet!

As for Groo the Goblin, he was so ashamed at being tricked by two imps that he packed up his things and he and Mrs. Groo disappeared, nobody knew where—and nobody minded, either!

The Lucky Fairy

HAVE you ever heard of the Lucky Fairy? If you haven't, I must tell you about her.

She lives in a tiny cottage just by the Lucky House, which is a queer sort of place. In the Lucky House grow hundreds of little Luck-charms, which fairies wear round their necks to bring them good luck.

I have never been inside the Lucky House, but I know all about it, so I will tell you what you would see if you peeped inside the door.

You would see a perfectly round room, with yellow shelves running all round it. On the shelves are put thousands of tiny pots, not much bigger than a thimble. The only window is in the roof, and through it the golden sun shines on to the little pots.

You would see a curious fire burning in the middle of the floor. There are no sticks, no coal to make it burn—there are just the flames springing up in four curling tongues. They are bright green in colour, and as they burn they send out a delicious scent, like nothing you can think of.

Sitting by the fire are four black cats, solemn and amber-eyed. At the beginning of every hour they take a grain of powder from a box by them, and throw it into the fire, which immediately springs up twice as high as before. Then the cats get up and walk gravely round this strange fire seven times. They sit down again, and wait for the next hour to come.

On the seventh day of the seventh month the cats go to the little pots and look at them. Then they see that very tiny green charms have grown up in them, and are ready for pulling. They are quite plain, oval in shape, and green in colour, and very, very tiny.

These are the good-luck charms that every fairy may have once a year if she has been good. They are very precious indeed, and as it is considered a dreadful thing to be without one, you may be sure that it is very seldom that any fairy has to be refused one. There are exactly the right number grown and on the seventh day of the seventh month all the fairies come to get one.

They put them on a slender silver chain and wear them round their necks, and then they need not fear bad spells, and will have good luck for a whole year. Nobody knows exactly how they grow, for no one but the cats and the Lucky Fairy are allowed inside the Lucky House.

The Lucky Fairy is the one who gives out the little Lucky charms. The fairies come to her cottage to get them, and show her a letter signed by the Fairy Queen to say they have been good, and then the Lucky Fairy gives them a new charm. She keeps one for herself, too, of course.

Now for years and years the Lucky Fairy had managed her work beautifully. It was not difficult. All she had to do was to fill four saucers with milk and take them to the black cats every day. She also had to water the little pots once a month. Then on the seventh day of the seventh month she had to go into the Lucky House and pull the little green charms from the pots and pop them into a basket ready to give them to the fairies.

It was very easy work, and she had plenty of time to go to dances, make herself pretty dresses of gossamer and petals, and talk to people who passed her way. She always had good luck, of course, because she wore her charm round her neck and didn't take it off day or night.

Then one day something happened.

A mouse went into the Lucky House. Nobody knows to this day how it got there. It smelt the delicious scent given off by the green flames, and thought it would go and see what it was. It might be a special kind of cheese, it might be fat bacon—it might even be both, the mouse thought.

So it went to see. The room was dark except for the green flames, for it was night-time, and the sun had gone. The little mouse didn't see the four black cats sitting still by the fire! It thought they were bits of furniture, they kept so very still. It went close to the fire, sniffing—and then something happened!

The cats all saw the daring little mouse at the same moment, and with a shrill *meow* they pounced on him. In the crowd of claws he somehow escaped, and whilst the cats were clawing about, meowing loudly, he ran up on to the first shelf of pots. He crouched behind one, though it didn't really hide him, and waited there, his tiny heart beating far too loudly.

Soon the cats found he wasn't by the fire, and they began to sniff round the room. When they came to the shelf where he was, they became very much excited, and sniffed all the more. Suddenly their shining eyes saw him, and they pounced. Over went the pots, and rolled to the floor. Some of them broke to bits, and the little green charms that were growing in them were trampled to nothing.

The mouse leapt to another shelf, and the cats followed. More pots were broken, but the cats cared nothing for that. All they wanted was that mouse.

But they didn't get him. He found a tiny crack in the roof by the window, and squeezed himself through it, leaving them meowing below. Then they suddenly saw the broken pots, and knew that some of the lucky charms were spoilt. What a dreadful thing! Some of the fairies would have to go without them! What *would* they say!

The cats were very much upset. They cleared up the mess, and counted the broken pots. There were twelve that were broken.

"We must tell the Lucky Fairy in the morning," said the biggest cat. "How many did you count were broken, each of you?"

"I counted twelve," said one cat.

"And I, too," said a second.

"And so did I," said a third.

"I did, too," said the biggest cat. "Four twelves are forty-eight. Oh dear!"

Now the cats didn't stop to think that they had all counted the *same* twelve, so that really they only needed to have twelve more pots. They quite thought that they must have forty-eight, and they told the Lucky Fairy this when she brought them their milk the next morning.

"Oh, Lucky Fairy," they said. "In the night a small mouse came, and when we chased it, forty-eight pots were broken. What is to be done about it? Forty-eight charms are destroyed."

"What a dreadful thing!" cried the Lucky Fairy. "It's never happened before. I must go to the Queen and ask her what must be done."

So she put on her new dress of red creeper leaves sewn with spider thread, and went to the Queen's court. She told Her Majesty what had happened, and asked what was to be done.

"I must have some more pots made at once,"

said the Queen, "and I must plant the lucky charm seeds in them myself. I have a few by me, which I have kept in case anything like this should happen. Forty-eight did you say?"

"Yes, Your Majesty," answered the fairy. "The cats counted the broken pots themselves."

Well, very fortunately, the Queen had enough seeds to spare, and with her own white hands she planted them in forty-eight tiny pots which the Court Potter made that very day for her.

"It is a good thing that there are still many months to go before the lucky charms will be given out," she said. "These will grow finely, I think, and be ready when the others are."

The pots were taken to the Lucky House, and the Lucky Fairy carefully placed them on the shelves. It was rather difficult to find room for them all, but she managed it. Then she gave the cats a good scolding, and told them that they were never to forget their duty again.

Time went by, and when the seventh day of the seventh month came round again, the cats told the Lucky Fairy that all the charms were ready to be given out.

"The forty-eight that the Queen planted have grown just as well as the others," they said. "So there will be just enough as usual."

All that day the fairies came crowding to the Lucky Fairy's cottage to get their new charms. They brought their letters with them to show that they had been good all the year round, and the Lucky Fairy was kept very busy handing out new charms from her full basket. She had pulled all the charms from the pots that morning, and had filled her basket to the very top.

When the evening came, her basket began to get empty. There were only about a hundred charms left. But the Lucky Fairy knew that some of the pixies might be late in coming to fetch theirs, for they had a good way to come. Sure enough, just as the sun was setting, she saw a little crowd of them come running through the wood towards her cottage.

"Sorry we're late," they panted, "but it's such a long way to come, and as the luck has just begun to wear out of our last year's charms, all sorts of silly things happened to prevent us coming quickly. Dinkie fell down and hurt his knee, and Pipkin lost his hat and had to go back for it. We shall be glad to have our *new* luck charms again, and then perhaps we shall be more fortunate on our way back."

The Lucky Fairy gave them all their new charms, and they hung them round their necks. Then they said good-bye and started back home. The Lucky Fairy looked down into her basket, and found she had still got some charms left.

"Hie!" she called after the pixies. "Are there any more of you to come?"

"No," they called back. "We're the last."

The Lucky Fairy looked down into her basket in astonishment. She counted the little green charms she had there, and found there were thirty-seven!

"Good gracious!" she said. "What a curious thing! I've never had any over before, except just my own new charm. If I take out my charm, I've still got thirty-six left. I wonder if everyone *has* been."

She stayed up very late that night, and listened to see if anyone else came to fetch a charm. But nobody did. Everybody had got one. In the morning the Lucky Fairy counted the charms again that she had over. She couldn't understand it. Then she suddenly gave a cry.

"Of course!" she said. "The cats must have counted wrongly. Because they all four counted twelve broken pots they must have thought there were four times twelve—forty-eight! The silly old things! I must take these extra ones back to the Queen."

She took her own charm, and slung it round her neck. Then a very naughty thought came into her head.

Why not keep *all* the extra charms for herself, and wear them round her neck, under her frock? No one would ever know, for only she herself knew that there were any over. What a lovely lot of good luck she would have if she did that!

The Lucky Fairy thought about this for such a long time that the four cats thought she had forgotten their milk. Soon she had made up her mind, and she quickly threaded all the thirty-six extra charms on her silver chain along with the charm she had already put there. Then she ran to fill the saucers with milk, and took them to the hungry cats.

It was not long before very good luck came to the Lucky Fairy. The next rainbow that came into the sky rested one of its ends just by her cottage. Of course, as you know, a crock of gold is always found at the rainbow's end, and when the Lucky Fairy saw it glittering so near she took her little spade and dug hard. Soon she came to a crock of gold, the biggest ever found at a rainbow's end, and this made her very rich!

Then, all in one week, six princes came riding by, and they each fell in love with her, and begged her to marry them. She felt that perhaps a king might come, so she said "No" to them all.

Not very long after that she found an old red ring, and when she rubbed it she found that she had got a wishing-ring! Could anything be luckier! The Lucky Fairy could now get everything she wanted! She was very proud and pleased, and at once wished a castle for herself, and a hundred little servants to do her bidding. She dressed in most wonderful dresses, and everyone was astonished at her good luck.

It didn't stop there, and soon people began to wonder how it was that the Lucky Fairy had such marvellous things happening to her. Then one day one of the black cats caught sight of the silver chain that the fairy wore, and saw, with his sharp eyes, all the many lucky charms on it. He thought about it for a day and a night, then he told the other three cats what he had seen.

"She has kept too many charms for herself," he said. "We must have counted wrongly that time we broke the pots."

They talked about it for a long time, and then they found out their mistake. Only twelve pots had been broken, not forty-eight. The naughty Lucky Fairy must have kept thirty-six extra charms for herself.

"To-morrow I will go to the Queen and tell her," said the biggest cat, solemnly. So after the Lucky Fairy had given him his saucer of milk, he walked out of the Lucky House and made his way to the Queen's court.

He told his story to her, and begged her pardon for having counted wrongly.

"But where are the extra lucky charms, then?" asked the Queen puzzled.

"The Lucky Fairy will know," said the cat. "She took all the charms from the pots as usual last time."

At once the Queen sent a message to the Lucky Fairy to go to her. She suddenly knew why the naughty little fairy had been so very, very lucky!

"What a dreadful thing to do, to take all the lucky charms for herself!" thought the Queen. "I must scold her very severely."

When the Lucky Fairy came to the palace the Queen sternly told her to take her silver chain from her neck. The fairy began to tremble, for she guessed that the Queen knew her secret. She took the chain from her neck and gave it to the Queen.

"I thought so," said the Queen, taking it. "You have kept far too many lucky charms for yourself! That was very dishonourable of you. I shall punish you."

"Please forgive me," begged the Lucky Fairy, beginning to cry. "I know it was wrong, and I'll never do it again."

"I shan't forgive you, unless you show me you are really sorry," said the Queen. "What will you do to prove that you are?"

"Oh, I don't know!" wept the Lucky Fairy. "I'll do anything! I'll give up all my lucky charms for a hundred years, if you like! But please let me still be the fairy who gives out the charms each year. I love my work, and I would hate not to do it. Please trust me still."

"Very well," said the Queen, "I will still trust you, but you must go without your own lucky charm every year, just to remind you of the naughty deed you have done. It won't hurt you to have a little bad luck for a change, after all the good fortune you have been having! And if ever there are any over again, you must not keep them, but you must give them to people who need them."

"Yes, Your Majesty," said the Lucky Fairy, drying her eyes. "Whom would you like me to give them to?"

"You might take them to the world of boys and girls," said the Queen. "There are lots of children who could do with a little good luck. You must find a good place to hide them in, so that only people who search for them may have them. Now go, and try to be good."

The Lucky Fairy went away feeling very much ashamed of herself. She wondered wherever she could hide the little green charms. She wandered on and on until she came to our world, and she sat down in a green meadow.

And there at her feet she saw green clover growing, with its three tiny leaves spreading out to the sun.

"Why, the leaves of this plant are exactly like my little green charms!" cried the fairy in surprise. "This would be a good place to hide them."

So she carefully fastened one of the charms on to a clover leaf. When she had finished, you couldn't tell which was charm and which was clover.

"A four-leaf clover!" she cried. "That shall be very lucky for whoever finds it! Now I'll go and find another patch of clover and hide another charm there, too."

Off she went, and very soon she had fastened all her charms on to clover leaves, making four-leaved clovers. When she had finished she flew back to her cottage, for she no longer had her castle, and vowed she would never do a naughty thing again.

Whether she did or not, I don't know, but every year she hides whatever lucky charms are over, in patches of clover, and makes the four-leaf clovers you sometimes find when you look hard enough.

And if you ever find one, do keep it, won't you, because it *may* bring you luck for a whole year. You won't know which of the leaves is the lucky charm from the Lucky House, but that doesn't matter—there's plenty of luck about it, if only you'll keep it!

The Enchanted Sea

ONE lovely sunny morning Jack and Mollie went out to play in their garden. It was a very big one, and at the end was a broad field.

"Let's go and play in the field this morning!" said Mollie. So down the garden they ran and opened the gate in the wall, meaning to run out into the green field.

But oh, what a surprise! There was no field there! Instead there was the blue sea—and how Mollie and Jack stared and stared!

"Mollie! What's happened?" asked Jack, rubbing his eyes. "Yesterday our field was here. To-day there's a big blue sea!"

"We must be dreaming," said Mollie. "Let's pinch each other, Jack, and if we each feel the pinch, we'll know we're *not* dreaming."

So they each pinched one another hard.

"Ooh!" they both cried. "Stop! You're hurting!"

"It's *not* a dream, it's real," said Jack, rubbing his arm. "But oh, Mollie! It must be magic or something. Let's go and tell Mummy."

They were just going to run back to the house when Mollie pointed to something on the smooth blue water.

"Look!" she said. "There's a boat coming— but isn't it a funny one?"

Jack looked. Yes, sure enough, it *was* a boat, a very strange one. It had high pointed ends, and at one end was a cat's head in wood and at the other a dog's head. A yellow sail billowed out in the wind.

"Who's in the boat?" said Jack. "It looks to me like a brownie or a gnome, Mollie."

"I feel a bit frightened," said Mollie. "Let's hide behind our garden wall, Jack, and peep over the top where the pear-tree is."

They ran behind the wall, climbed the pear-tree and then, hidden in its leafy branches, peeped over the top. They saw the boat come nearer and nearer, and at last it reached the shore. Out jumped the brownie, threw a rope round a wooden post near by, and then ran off into the wood to the left of the children's garden.

"Well, that was one of the fairy folk for certain!" said Jack, in excitement. "Did you see his pointed hat and shoes and long beard, Mollie?"

For a long time the children watched, but the

little brownie did not come back. After a bit Jack began to long to see the boat more closely, so he and Mollie climbed down the pear-tree and ran quietly over the grass to where the boat lay rocking gently.

"Oh, Mollie, it *must* be a magic one!" said Jack. "Do let's get in it just for a moment to see what it feels like! Think how grand it will be to tell everyone we have sat in a brownie's boat!"

So the two children clambered into the little boat and sat down on the wooden seat in the middle. And then a dreadful thing happened!

The rope round the post suddenly uncoiled itself and slipped into the boat. The wind blew hard and the yellow sail billowed out. The boat rocked from end to end, and off it went over the queer enchanted sea!

"Ooh!" said Mollie, frightened. "Jack! What shall we do? The boat's sailing away with us!"

But Jack could do nothing. The wind blew them steadily over the water, and their garden wall grew smaller and smaller, the farther away they sailed.

"That brownie *will* be cross to find his boat gone," said Mollie, almost crying. "Where do you suppose it's taking us?"

On and on went the little boat, the dog's head pointing forwards and the cat's head backwards. Mollie looked at the back of the dog's head, and thought that it looked a little like their dog at home.

"I do wish we had our dear old Rover with

us," she said. "I'm sure he would be a great help."

To her great surprise the wooden dog's head pricked up its ears and the head turned round and looked at her.

"If you are fond of dogs, *I* shall be pleased to help you," it said.

"You *did* give us a fright!" said Jack, almost falling off his seat in surprise. "Are you magic?"

"Yes, and so is the wooden cat over there," said the dog. "We're only wooden figureheads, but there's plenty of good magic about us. You look nice little children, and if you are fond of animals and kind to them, the cat and I will be very glad to help you."

"Meeow!" said the cat's head, and it turned round and smiled at the two astonished children.

"Well, first of all, can you tell us about this strange sea?" asked Jack. "It's never been here before."

"Oh yes, it has, but usually at night-time when nobody is about to see it," said the dog. "It belongs to the Wizard High-Hat. He sent his servant, the brownie Tick-a-tock, to fetch a red-and-yellow toadstool from the wood near your garden and made the sea stretch from his island to there, so that Tick-a-tock could sail quickly there and back."

"But I expect he lay down and fell asleep," said the cat. "He's always doing that. So when you got into the boat, it sailed off with you instead of the brownie. It doesn't know the difference between you, you see."

"Oh goodness!" said Jack, in a fright. "Does that mean it's taking us to the Wizard High-Hat?"

"Yes," said the dog, "and he'll be in a fine temper when he sees you instead of the brownie!"

"Whatever shall we do?" said Mollie, looking anxiously round to see if the wizard's island was anywhere in sight.

"Well, we might be able to help you, if you'll just say a spell over us to make us come properly alive when we get to the island," said the dog. "If we were a proper dog and cat we could perhaps protect you."

"What is the spell?" asked Jack.

"One of you must stroke my head, and the other must pat the cat's head," said the dog, looking quite excited. The cat mewed loudly and blinked her green eyes. "Then you must say the magic word I'll whisper into your ear, and stamp seven times on the bottom of the boat. Then you'll see what happens when we reach the shore. Don't do any of these things till we reach the island."

The dog whispered the magic word into each child's ear, and they repeated it again and again to themselves to make sure they had it right. Then suddenly Mollie pointed in front of the boat.

"Look!" she said. "There's the island—and, oh my! Is that the wizard's palace on that hill in the middle?"

"Yes," said the dog. "You'll see some of his soldiers in a minute. They always meet the boat."

Sure enough the children saw six little soldiers come marching out of the palace gates towards the shore. They were dressed in red, and looked very like Jack's wooden soldiers at home.

The boat sailed nearer and nearer to the shore, and the dog told Jack and Mollie to use the spell he had taught them. So Jack stroked the dog's head, Mollie patted the cat's head, and each of them said the magic word, and then stamped loudly on the bottom of the boat seven times.

And what a surprise they had! Each wooden head grew legs and a body, and hey presto, a live cat and dog jumped down from the ends of the boat and frisked round the children in delight!

"We're real, we're real!" they cried. "Now we can go with you and help you."

The boat grounded on the sandy shore and the rope flew out and tied itself round a post. The chief of the soldiers stepped up and looked most astonished to see the two children.

"Where's Tick-a-tock the brownie?" he asked, sternly. "What are you doing here?"

"Well, you see, we stepped into the brownie's boat and it sailed off with us," said Jack. "We're very sorry, and please would you ask the wizard to excuse us and send the boat back to our garden to take us home again?"

"You must come and ask him yourself," said the soldier. "You are very naughty children!"

The six soldiers surrounded Jack and Mollie and marched them off towards the palace on the hill. The dog and cat followed behind, and the soldiers took no notice of them.

Soon the children were mounting the long flight

of steps up to the castle, and were pushed into a large hall, where sat the Wizard High-Hat on a silver throne. He looked most surprised when he saw Jack and Mollie, and at once demanded to know how they got there.

Jack told him, and he frowned.

"Now that is most annoying," he said crossly. "I want to send my sea to another place to-morrow, and that means that Tick-a-tock won't get back with the toadstool. I shall keep you prisoner here for a hundred years, unless you can do the things I tell you to do."

Mollie began to cry, and Jack turned pale.

"Please don't set us very hard tasks," he said. "I'm only eight years old, and Mollie's only seven, and doesn't know her six times table yet."

The wizard laughed scornfully, and commanded his soldiers to take the children to the bead-room. They were led to a small room with a tiny window set high up. On the floor were thousands and thousands of beads of all colours and sizes.

"Now," said the wizard, "your first task is to sort out all these beads into their different colours and sizes. You can have to-day and to-night to do this in, and if you haven't finished by to-morrow morning you shall be my prisoners for a hundred years."

With that he closed the door with a bang, and he and his soldiers tramped away. The children looked at one another in dismay.

"We can never do that!" said Mollie, in despair.

"Why, it would take us *weeks* to sort out all these beads!"

"Where are the cat and dog?" asked Jack looking all round. "They don't seem to be here. They might have helped us."

Suddenly the door opened again, and the dog and cat were flung into the room, panting. Then the door closed again, and the four were prisoners.

"We thought we wouldn't be able to get to you!" said the dog. "So I bit a soldier on the leg and the cat scratched another on the hand, and they were so angry that they threw us in here with you!"

"Just see what we've got to do!" said Mollie, in despair, and she pointed to the beads. "We've got to sort out all these before to-morrow morning."

"My word!" said the dog, blowing out his whiskered cheeks. "That's a dreadful job! Come, Puss! Let's all set to work."

The four began to sort out the beads, and for an hour they worked steadily. Then the door opened and a soldier put a loaf of bread, a bone, a jug of water and a saucer of milk into the room. Then the door shut and the key was turned.

The children ate the bread and drank the water. The dog gnawed the bone and the cat drank the milk.

"It's no use going on with these beads," said the cat, suddenly. "We shall never get them done. *I* know what I'll do!"

"What?" asked the children, excitedly.

"You wait and see!" said the cat, and she

finished her milk. Then she washed herself. After that she went round the little room, and looked hard at every hole in the wall.

"Now watch!" she said. She sat down in the middle of the floor and began to make a curious squeaking noise that sounded like a thousand mice squealing at once—and a very curious thing happened!

Out of the mouse-holes round the room there came running hundreds of little brown mice. They scampered to where the cat sat, and made ring after ring round her. When about a thousand mice were there, the cat stopped making the queer noise and glared at the mice.

"I could eat you all!" she said, in a frightening voice. "But if you will do something for me, I will set you free!"

She pointed to the beads. "Sort those out into different colours and sizes!" she said. "And be quick about it!"

At once the thousand mice scuttled to the beads. Each mouse chose a bead of a certain colour and size and carefully put it to start a pile. Soon the little piles grew and grew, and the big pile sank to nothing. In half an hour all the thousands of beads were neatly sorted out into hundreds of piles of beads, all of different colours and sizes.

"Good!" said the cat to the trembling mice. "You may go!"

Off scampered the mice to their holes and disappeared. The children hugged the clever cat, and thanked her.

"Now we'll let the wizard know his task is done!" said the cat. "Kick the door, Jack."

Jack kicked the door and an angry soldier opened it.

"Tell the wizard we've finished our work," said Jack, and the soldier gaped in astonishment to see the neat piles of beads. He fetched the wizard, who could hardly believe his eyes.

"Take them to the Long Field!" said High-Hat to his soldiers. So the children, followed by the cat and dog, were taken to a great field which was surrounded on all sides by high fences. The grass in this field was very long, almost up to the children's knees.

"Here is a pair of scissors for each of you," said the wizard, with a cunning smile. "Cut this grass for me before morning, or I will keep you prisoner for a hundred years!"

The children looked at the scissors in dismay. They were very small, and the grass was so long and there was such a lot of it! The wizard and his soldiers shut the gate of the field and left the four alone together.

"Well, I don't know what we're going to do *this* time!" said Jack, beginning to cut the grass with his scissors, "but it seems to me we're beaten!"

He and Mollie cut away for about an hour, but at the end of that time their hands were so tired, and they had cut so small a patch of grass that they knew it was of no use going on. They would never even get a tenth of the field cut by the morning.

"Can't you think of something clever to help us again?" asked Jack at last, turning to the cat and dog.

"We're both thinking hard," said the cat. "I believe the dog has an idea. Don't disturb him for a minute."

The dog was lying down, frowning. Mollie and Jack kept very quiet. Suddenly the dog jumped up and ran to Mollie.

"Feel round my collar," he said to her. "You'll find a little wooden whistle there."

Mollie soon found the whistle, and the dog put it into his mouth. Then he began to whistle very softly. The sound was like the wind in the grass, the drone of bees and the tinkling of far-away water.

Suddenly, holes appeared in the earth all around the high fence, and hundreds of grey rabbits peeped out of them. They had dug their way into the field under the fence, and as soon as they saw the dog blowing on his magic whistle, they ran up to him and sat down in rings round him. He took the whistle from his mouth and looked at them.

"I chase rabbits!" he said. "But I will let you go free if you will do something for me. Do you see this beautiful green, juicy grass? Eat it as quickly as you can, and you shall go the way you came."

At once the rabbits set to work nibbling the green grass. It was very delicious and they enjoyed it. In an hour's time the whole field was as smooth as velvet, and not a blade of grass was longer than Mollie's little finger.

"Good!" said the dog to the rabbits. "You may go!"

At once they scampered away. Jack ran to the gate in the fence and hammered on it. The wizard himself opened it, and when he saw the smooth field, with all the long grass gone, he gasped in astonishment.

"Where's the grass you cut?" he asked at last, looking here and there.

The children didn't know what to say, so they didn't answer. The wizard grew angry, and called his soldiers.

"Take them to the topmost room of my palace and lock them in!" he roared. "They have been using magic! Well, they'll find themselves somewhere where they can't use magic now!"

In half a minute the soldiers surrounded the children and animals again and hustled them back to the palace. Up hundreds and hundreds of stairs they took them, and at last, right at the very top, they came to a room that was locked. The wizard took a key from his girdle and unlocked it. The children and animals were pushed inside and the door was locked on the outside.

By this time it was almost night-time. A tiny lamp burnt high up in the ceiling. There was one window, but it was barred across. Jack looked round in despair.

"Well, I don't see what we can do now!" he said, with a sigh! "I'm afraid, cat and dog, that even you, clever though you are, can't do anything to help us."

The dog and cat prowled all round the room, but the walls were strong and thick, and the door was locked fast. For a long time the four sat on the floor together, then suddenly the cat jumped up and ran to the window.

"Open it!" she said. "I want to see if I can squeeze through the bars."

Mollie and Jack opened the heavy window, and the cat jumped lightly on to the ledge.

"What's the good of squeezing through the bars?" asked Jack, peering down. "You could never jump down, Puss! Why, we're right at the very top of the palace!"

The cat squeezed through the bars and stood on the outer window-ledge. Her green eyes shone in the darkness.

"There's another window-ledge nearby!" she whispered. "I will jump on to that, and see if the window there is open. If it is, I'll go in, and see if I can find some way of helping you all to escape!"

With that she jumped neatly to the next window-ledge, and disappeared. The window there *was* open and the brave cat leapt lightly into the room. The palace was in darkness. Wizard, soldiers and servants were all sleeping. The soft-footed cat ran down the stairs, and at last reached a room from which loud snores came. She ran in, and by the light of a small candle saw the wizard asleep on his bed. On the table near the candle lay his keys!

In a trice the cat had them in her mouth and back she went up the stairs, leapt on to the window-ledge, and then jumped on to the next ledge, mewing to the children as she jumped. How excited they were to see the keys!

Jack fitted them one by one into the lock of the door until he found the right one. He turned it, and the door opened! Quietly the two children, the cat and the dog slipped down the hundreds of stairs, and undid the heavy palace door. Out they went into the moonlight, and ran down to the seashore.

"I do hope the sea still stretches to our garden wall," said Jack. "Hurry up, little boat, and take us home again."

The boat set off over the water. Suddenly Mollie gave a cry and pointed to each end of the boat. The dog and cat had disappeared, and once more the two wooden figure heads stood high at each end.

"The magic is gone from them!" said Mollie. "Oh, I do hope they don't mind. They've gone back to being wooden heads again."

"Don't you worry about us," said the dog. "We've enjoyed our adventure, and we're quite happy. I only hope the boat will take you home again."

On and on sailed the little ship in the bright moonlight. After a long time Jack caught Mollie's arm and pointed.

"Our garden wall!" he said, in delight.

"Who's that on the edge of the sea?" asked Mollie, seeing a little figure standing there.

"It must be Tick-a-tock the brownie!" said Jack.

"How pleased he will be to see his boat coming back again. I expect he thought he was quite lost."

The boat touched the grass, and the children jumped out. They called good-bye to the dog and cat, and then felt themselves pushed aside. The brownie had rushed up to his boat, and leapt in as quickly as he could. The sails filled out and off went the boat in the moonlight, the dog barking and the cat mewing in farewell.

"That's the end of a most exciting adventure," said Jack. "Goodness, I wonder what Mummy has been thinking all this time! We'll tell her about our adventure, and in the morning perhaps Daddy will make us a raft and we can all go exploring on the magic sea."

Mummy *was* glad to see them. She had been so worried. She could hardly believe her ears when she heard all that had happened.

"You must go to bed now," she said. "But to-morrow we'll all go down to see the enchanted water, and perhaps Daddy will sail off to the wizard's island to punish him for keeping you prisoner."

But in the morning the sea was gone! Not a single sign of it was left—there were only green fields and hills stretching far away into the distance. The wizard had called his sea back again, and although Jack and Mollie have watched for it to return every single day, it never has. Isn't it a pity?

The Little Penny-Purse

ONCE upon a time there was a little girl called Tessie who lived with her mother in a tiny cottage. They were very poor indeed, and both Tessie and her mother had to work hard to earn enough money to buy bread and meat.

Their cottage was very clean but very poor. Their clothes were neatly mended, but so old that they were more darns than cloth. The only pretty things that Tessie had were a pair of shoe buckles. They were of bright silver and had little stones set in them here and there. They had belonged to Tessie's grandmother, and her mother had given them to her little girl one Christmas-time.

Tessie was very proud of the buckles. She wore them once a year on her birthday, and was very careful not to lose them. She used to look at her shoes every other minute to make sure that her buckles were still there.

One day, when Tessie and her mother had been working very hard indeed for weeks, the mother fell ill. She had to go to bed, and poor Tessie found her day very full indeed, for she had to try and do enough work for both.

"If only I could get rich!" she thought. "Then I would take Mother away to the seaside and get her quite better. I would buy her a new dress and a lovely new hat. But oh dear, there isn't even enough money to get our old shoes mended!"

That day there came a letter for Tessie. She was very much excited, for letters hardly ever came to their little cottage. When she opened it, she gave a cry of delight.

"Oh Mother!" she said. "This is an invitation from the farmer's wife, Mrs. Straws, to ask me to a picnic party she is giving to all the boys and girls around. Oh, if only I could go!"

"Well, you shall!" said her mother. "You have been working far too hard, and you need a treat. You must go, Tessie."

"But what about my dreadful old shoes?" asked Tessie. "How can I go in those, Mother?"

"You must sew your pretty buckles on them," said her mother. "Then no one will notice the old shoes. They will look at the buckles instead. But you must be very careful not to lose them, Tessie."

"Oh, I will!" said the little girl, very happy to think that she was going to a picnic and was going to wear her lovely buckles too. She straightway got her needle and cotton and sewed the buckles on the shoes. They did look lovely.

The picnic was the next day. Tessie washed and ironed her only frock, brushed her hair, and put on her shoes. Then she kissed her mother good-bye.

"See that you bring both buckles back safely!" called her mother, as Tessie danced out of the door.

The picnic was lovely. There were cakes and sandwiches, chocolates and apples. There were all sorts of games. Tessie ran about and laughed and shouted gaily. She forgot all about her shoe-buckles for a long time, and then she hurriedly looked at her feet.

The buckles were there—but one of them was coming loose! Oh bother! Tessie really couldn't go and ask at the farmhouse for a needle and thread. Perhaps the buckle would stay on safely till she got home.

There were prizes for the girl or boy who could run the fastest, and to Tessie's great delight she won a lovely doll. She could hardly believe her good luck! She longed to race home and show her mother what she had won.

When the picnic came to an end Tessie took her doll and ran home through the wood. Suddenly she felt something slip off her shoe, and she looked down—one of the buckles was gone!

"Oh well!" said Tessie. "It's only just this minute slipped off, so I'll easily find it."

But she didn't look very hard for she was so anxious to run home and show her mother the lovely doll.

"I'll put a stick just here, then I'll come back and find it to-morrow," she thought. "Nobody comes this way but me, so it will be quite safe."

She took a big twig and stuck it in the ground just where she had felt the buckle slip off her shoe. Then off she ran again.

"Look, Mother!" she cried, rushing into the room where her mother lay in bed. "See what I have won at the picnic! Isn't it a beautiful doll? I shall call her Josephine."

"It is lovely," said her mother. Then she looked at Tessie's shoes, and saw at once that a buckle was missing.

"Where's that buckle?" she asked. "Surely you haven't been so naughty as to lose it, Tessie!"

"Oh, it slipped off my shoe in the wood and I thought I would go and find it to-morrow," said Tessie. "I know just about where it is, Mother. It's quite safe."

"You naughty little girl!" cried her mother. "I shouldn't have let you wear those beautiful buckles if I had known you would be so careless. You certainly will not leave the lost one till to-morrow. You will go this minute and find it now."

But it was getting dark by that time, so it was of no use to go to the wood. Tessie was well scolded, and she cried and said that she would go early in the morning to the wood.

So the next day, very early, she set off. In her pocket was the little wooden box in which the buckles were kept. Only one was there, but Tessie hoped to go home with both.

She soon came to the part of the wood where she had left the twig stuck into the ground. Then she began to hunt around. She hadn't been hunting long before she saw someone else doing just the same thing—hunting here, and hunting there— peering beneath leaves, and parting the thick grasses.

It was a brownie, a little man about the same size as Tessie. He had a long beard and kindly twinkling eyes. Tessie knew that there were fairy folk in the wood but she had never seen any before, and she looked in delight at the little man.

"What are you looking for?" she asked.

"For a shoe buckle," answered the brownie.

"Oh, how funny!" cried Tessie. "So am I!"

They both went on hunting and hunting, but neither could find what they were looking for.

"What is your buckle like?" asked Tessie.

"Like this," said the brownie, and he showed Tessie a buckle exactly like the one she had lost. "What is yours like?"

"Like this!" said Tessie, and she opened the little box in which she had the other buckle. The two stared at one another in surprise.

"I lost my buckle here yesterday," said Tessie, "and Mother was very cross with me and sent me back to look for it. She says I mustn't come back till I've found it. When did you lose yours?"

"Well, to tell you the truth, I haven't lost one," said the brownie. "I found this one just here

142

yesterday, and as it was very pretty, I thought perhaps I should find the other if I looked very hard. You see, there is a tea-party at the Red Gnome's to-day, and I longed to wear some pretty buckles on my new shoes."

"Oh!" said Tessie. "Then you must have found *my* buckle! And I've been looking and looking for it! Will you give it back to me, please?"

"Oh no, do let me keep it," begged the brownie. "Please give me the other one, then I shall have two. *Do* be a kind little girl and let me have the buckles. You have no idea how well they go with my new shoes."

"But Mother will be so angry," said Tessie, the tears coming into her eyes.

Still the brownie begged and pleaded, and at last Tessie's kind heart made her say yes, he could have them both. So she handed over the box with the other buckle in, and the brownie thanked her very much.

"Here is something in exchange," he said. "It is nothing much—just a little penny-purse. Please keep it."

Tessie took it, said "thank you," and ran off. She knew that her mother would scold her, and she cried all the way home.

Sure enough, when her mother heard what she had done, she was very cross indeed.

"Fancy taking a stupid little penny-purse instead of your lovely buckles!" she cried. "Give it to me, you silly little girl!"

Tessie gave the tiny purse to her. It was very

small, just big enough to hold a penny. Her mother emptied the penny on to the table, and then tossed the purse to Tessie.

"That's all you've got for your buckles!" she said. "A penny and a stupid little purse that is no use for anything."

Tessie picked up the purse—and to her surprise it felt as if there was something hard in it. She opened it, and inside there lay another penny!

"Oh, Mother!" she said. "There were two pennies, not one. Look, you didn't take out this one."

She put it on the table beside the other—and then looked at the purse in surprise—for she could feel something hard and round in it again! She opened it and there lay another penny! Tessie could hardly believe her eyes!

"Why, it's magic!" she said. "Every time we take a penny out, another one comes! Look, Mother, here's a third penny!"

"Well, the purse must be magic then," said her mother, in delight. "See here's a fourth penny—and now I've taken that out, a fifth penny has appeared in the little purse! Oh my, Tessie, what a fine gift! This is better than a pair of buckles!"

All the morning long Tessie and her mother took pennies out of the little penny-purse. The table was piled with the round brown coins and a big chest was full to the brim. As fast as they took out one penny another came!

"Our fortunes are made!" cried Tessie's mother. "Take a bagful of the pennies to the post-mistress and ask her to let you have some shillings for them."

So off went Tessie and exchanged a big bag of pennies for thirty bright shillings. How pleased and excited she was!

"I shall be able to get a doctor for Mother," she thought. "And lots of new clothes. And we'll have a holiday by the sea. What fun it will be! Oh what a good thing I let the little brownie have my shoe-buckles!"

Everything happened as Tessie planned. The doctor said that a seaside holiday would make her mother quite better, so off they went one day together in brand new clothes, as happy as could be. In Tessie's pocket was the little penny-purse—she wasn't going to lose sight of that, you may be sure!

As for the brownie, he was never sorry that he had parted with his penny-purse, for everyone admired the buckles on his new shoes, and he felt very proud indeed. He wears them to this day, and they are just as bright and pretty as ever they were!

The Little Girl who told Stories

ONCE upon a time there was a little girl called Rosaline. She was a pretty little thing, with beautiful manners and a kind heart; but dear me, she told the most dreadful stories! She hardly ever kept to the truth, and her poor mother really didn't know how to cure her.

She would say that she had seen a parrot in the garden, when she had seen nothing but a little brown sparrow. She vowed that she was top girl in her class at school when really she was only fifth. She told her friends that she had twenty glorious frocks in her cupboard at home, when she had only four quite ordinary ones and one silk party frock.

So you can see what a dreadful little story-teller she was! It wasn't a bit of good Rosaline being

kind and pretty, because she always spoilt everything by telling untruths.

One day she wandered into Wishing Wood,
which was just near her home. She found a little
path she had never seen before, and she ran down
it, wondering where it went. After about half an
hour she came to the funniest little house she had
ever seen.

It was like a small hillock, about half as high
again as Rosaline. Daisies grew thickly all over it,
and it was a very pretty sight. In one side was a
bright yellow door, with a blue knocker.

"Well!" said Rosaline, stopping in surprise.
"What a very peculiar little house! I wonder who
lives in it?"

She very soon knew, for at that moment the
yellow door flew open, and a small man came out.
He looked very much worried, and he beckoned to
Rosaline.

"Can you cut thin sandwiches?" he asked.

Rosaline looked astonished. Then she nodded her
head.

"Yes," she said. "I often cut them for Mummy
when we're going picnicking."

"Well, *do* come in and help me cut some,"
begged the little man. "I seem to be making such
a mess of it."

Rosaline followed him into the queer house.
It was perfectly round inside, and the furniture
was very small. On a little table was a big loaf of
bread, a dish of butter, and a jar of home-made
potted meat.

"It's like this," said the dwarf. "I've been asked to a picnic to-day, and I promised to take some sandwiches. But I've never made any before, and so I can't seem to cut them nicely."

Rosaline looked at the big pieces he had hacked off the loaf and tried to spread with butter.

"Yes, they are not very nice," she said. "Never mind, I'll do as many as you want."

She asked him for a sharp knife, and then set to work. She was neat and quick with her hands, and soon had a fine pile of thin, well-buttered sandwiches on a plate. When she had made twenty, the little man told her that was enough.

"They are beautifully made!" he said gratefully. "Thank you so much. Now I should like to give you something in return for your kindness."

"Oh, no, that's quite all right," said Rosaline politely.

"It would please me very much to give you a nice present," said the little man. "Come with me, and you shall choose something for yourself."

He lifted up a trap-door in the floor, and Rosaline saw a flight of steps leading downwards. The dwarf led the way and she followed. They went along a dark passage lit dimly by an old hanging lantern, and then came to a big cave. In it were sitting many other little men, all hard at work.

"What are they doing?" whispered Rosaline.

"Look and see," answered the little man.

She bent over the busy dwarfs and saw that they were making all kinds of marvellous jewellery.

Green precious stones, blue ones, yellow, white, and red, every colour was there, and each stone was being set into wonderful glittering necklaces, bracelets, rings, and brooches.

"Oh, how lovely!" cried Rosaline, as she saw them. "I never did see anything quite so beautiful as your lovely stones, little man!"

"Well, I'm pleased to hear you say so," said the dwarf, smiling. "Now just choose anything you think you would like, and I shall be delighted to give it to you. One good turn deserves another."

"You *are* kind," said Rosaline, going red with delight. "I haven't a ring, so do you think I might choose one?"

"Certainly," said the little man. "What colour?"

"Well, I have such a pretty green frock at home that I think I'd like a green one to match," said Rosaline.

At once one of the dwarfs ran over to her with a tray of bright green rings. Rosaline picked one up and looked at it. It was set in silver, and the green stone was very big and bright.

"May I have this one?" she asked.

"Yes," said the dwarf. "But I must just warn you of something, Rosaline, if you have that ring. Never tell an untruth whilst you are wearing it, for it can only belong to someone truthful."

"Oh, I'll be very careful," said Rosaline. She slipped the ring on her finger, and then followed the dwarf along the passage back to his little house again. She thanked him very much, said good-bye, and ran home, delighted with her present. The ring shone brightly on her finger, and was so beautiful that it caught everyone's eye.

Now the next day, when Rosaline went to school, all the girls and boys crowded round her to see the ring, for they soon noticed it on her finger.

"Where did you get it, where did you get it?" they cried.

Rosaline told them her story—but alas! she could not keep to the truth.

"The little man wanted a hundred sandwiches," she said, "and I cut them all in five minutes. Wasn't it clever of me? No wonder he wanted to give me a ring!"

Suddenly Rosaline gave a cry. The ring suddenly seemed to become much tighter, and pressed so hard round her finger that it hurt her.

"Oh, Rosaline!" cried the children. "Your ring has changed colour! Look! It has gone a fiery red colour! How queer!"

So it had. It had lost its beautiful bright green hue, and was now a flaming, angry red. It was so tight that Rosaline couldn't get it off, and it hurt her very much.

Suddenly one of the children pointed his finger at her.

"I know, I know!" he cried. "You've told a story and the ring's gone red for danger! Story-teller, story-teller!"

Rosaline went as red as the ring. She suddenly remembered the dwarf's warning, and she knew she had been foolish and wrong.

"I—I *did* tell a story," she said humbly. "I only made twenty sandwiches, not a hundred."

At once the ring stopped squeezing her finger, and became its proper size. It went dark for a moment, and then turned from red to its own bright green once again.

"It's green again, it's green again!" cried everyone. Rosaline looked at it in astonishment. What a peculiar ring!

"I don't think I like it very much, after all," she thought. "It will be dreadful if it keeps turning red like that."

The ring remained green all that day, and then Rosaline forgot again. Her mother said it must be bedtime, and sent Rosaline to see if it was half-past six.

It was, but Rosaline didn't want to go to bed. So the naughty little girl told her mother that it was only ten minutes past the hour. No sooner had she told that story than the ring tightened on her finger again, and made her cry out. It went fiery red, and Rosaline, frightened that her mother might see it, hastily told the truth.

"No, Mummy, I made a mistake," she said. "It *is* half-past six, so I'd better go to bed."

The ring loosened, and became green once more. Rosaline kissed her mother good night, and ran off.

That night in bed she had a long think. She wanted to wear the ring, for it was very beautiful, but she knew quite well that she could only do so safely if she stopped telling stories.

"Well, it *is* horrid to keep telling stories," thought

the little girl. "I'd better stop, before I get too bad. And the ring will help me, for every time I feel it hurting me, I'll know I've not spoken truly, and I'll own up."

She fell asleep comforted. But although it was easy to make up her mind to be good, it was dreadfully hard to get out of her bad habit. Rosaline was horrified to find how many times she told stories. Time after time she felt the ring tighten angrily on her finger, and saw it change to a fierce red, attracting everyone's attention to it.

"Story-teller, story-teller!" cried the children when they saw the ring change colour. "Oh, you naughty little story-teller!"

Then Rosaline would go red, too, and say she was sorry, and tell the truth properly. The ring would flash green again, whilst the children laughed. But little by little Rosaline learnt her lesson, and soon she became quite a truthful little girl.

She still has the ring, and if ever you meet her she will show it to you, and perhaps let you wear it for a few minutes. But if you are a story-teller, don't put it on—for the ring will turn a fiery red, and so will you!